VALHALLA'S DOOM

THE SELA HELSDATTER SAGA
BOOK FOUR

RORI BLEU

ROSIE CHAPEL

First printing: 2024
ISBN: 978-0-6459731-9-8 (eBook)
ISBN: 978-1-7635407-0-5 (Paperback)

Ulfire Pty. Ltd.
P.O. Box 1481
South Perth
WA 6951
Australia

Cover Design: R Norman

Cover Image: Canva
Designed in Canva
Internal images: Canva/Deposit Photos.
Created using appropriate licences.

❀ Created with Vellum

Acknowledgment
RORI BLEU

I would like to thank Kirsten Miller, Annette Begeschke, and Becky Avery for hounding... err... I mean encouraging me to write this book and finish the series. You were right, Anna needed her story told.

I would also like to thank my co-author and editor, Rosie Chapel. You did an awesome job giving the series the love it needed to be a complete storyline.

And who would have thought we'd get the side story out before the series finale?

Acknowledgment
ROSIE CHAPEL

Shortly after we finished Freya's story, a novella which runs parallel with books two to four of this saga, I lost my Dad.

Grief is a fickle mistress and, for a while, she stole my inspiration. I could not summon up the will to write, and started to question whether this was more than just writer's block induced by shock.

After giving me the space I needed, and then some, Rori badgered me (this is the politest term to describe her insistence) to read the beginning of Anna's story, just to check it was on the right track, she assured — no pressure...

She knows me too well and, although it took a little longer for the spark to take hold, I'm so glad she did not give up on me.

Thank you, Rori.

VALHALLA'S DOOM

The Sela Helsdatter Saga
Book Four

Rori Bleu

Rosie Chapel

PROLOGUE

T hunderously mocking laughter captured Loki's attention, and he raised his eyes to the roof of the cave.

"Come down here, coward, and let's end this," Loki bawled.

Odin's reply — a hailstorm of energy.

Loki readied himself for the punishing fury, only to have his feet knocked out from under him by a slender body. He reeled across the floor like a drunkard, and fell flat on his back.

Winded, he blinked, his gaze landing on Sela's delicate countenance.

"Must I save your cute butt every time, *ástin mín*?" She smiled at him. Being able to call Loki *my love* again, fueled her determination to end Odin. Brushing a kiss to his lips, she planted the palms of her hands on his chest and pushed herself upright.

Loki was surprised — although why eluded him, this was Sela after all — when her swords materialized in her hands. *Wait... no...* awe supplanted surprise as he registered it was more than that; her hands had actually *become* the swords.

He intended to ask her *how* she managed that trick, but this was not the time.

He followed his wife, and the pair confronted Odin. Savagely, Sela slashed at the Asgardian's face. One of her blades sliced his left ear from his head.

"You two are the bane of my existence," Odin sneered and, seizing Sela as though she was nothing but a ragdoll, threw her at Loki. "Your deaths will be like sunlight after the storm.

The couple toppled to the ground, jarring Jörmungandr's head.

Their combined weight caused the serpent's grip on his tail to falter. He struggled to maintain his grasp, deepening his bite. His body arched violently against the chains, sending powerful shockwaves through the Earth's crust.

Spying cracks developing in the stone cavern, Odin concocted a new battle plan.

Ignoring Loki and Sela, he switched his attack to the World Serpent, concentrating his magic on the gaping wound at Jörmungandr's tail. He doubled his efforts when he saw the flesh begin to cleave in two.

Without warning, Odin felt himself being yanked from the air. Arms cartwheeling, he could not stop his downwards plunge and slammed onto the stone floor.

Heaving himself to his feet, he soared again, only to suffer a repeat performance.

Slow to rise this time, his infuriated gaze sought out Sela and Loki, bracing himself to destroy them both for daring to assault him, baffled to see the pair preoccupied with trying to save the mangled remains of Jörmungandr's tail.

That was when his focus darted to the diminutive, glowing figure in front of him. Red eyes, brimming with loathing, stared down the All Father.

"I think you will discover the bane of your sorry existence is me," Anna's pure, bell-like tones, in stark contrast with the venom emanating from her prey.

"Nature and Magic have judged you guilty of abusing your gifts, Odin of Asgard," she pronounced judgment in the most ancient of tongues.

"There will be no mercy for you, Old Man. Your death will be complete, and your existence will be wiped from memory."

"No." Terror clawed at Odin upon hearing the sentence. "How dare you speak to me with such blatant disrespect, girl?" he objected strenuously.

"I am Odin of Asgard. I am all magic. A pitiful creature such as you cannot possibly possess the power to destroy me. No one does. Your pathetic family will never know peace," he threatened for good measure.

Incandescent with rage, Odin summoned all his power, and cast it at the insolent urchin, satisfied when Anna vanished in a towering tempest.

Rising to his feet, he prepared to rid the Realms of her parents as well.

"Is that the best you have, Asgardian?" The angry voice boomed from within the stormy mass.

Stupefied, Odin watched the brat absorb the blast and emerge unscathed. He scrambled to bombard her with another volley.

Too late.

Anna stretched her arms out in front of her and clenched her hands together in a death grip.

Odin glanced down at his sides, feeling his arms being crushed under a tremendous, invisible pressure.

Convinced Anna had summoned creatures from whatever pit of Helheim, she had crawled out of, he was appalled to realize, it was the child herself who controlled his fate.

Reduced to begging for his life, Odin screeched a painful pledge, "I-I believe in your strength, child. Spare me, and I will grant you anything you want; untold wealth, and dominion over all Realms but Asgard."

Closing her eyes, Anna silenced his shrieks.

Slowly, her eyes opened and focused on his chest. "Your immortality has been rescinded by your malfeasance."

Her proclamation echoed with a strange dissonance, at odds with her usual melodic tones.

Odin, the All-Father, once the most honorable, the most noble, and the most wise was doomed.

"Was it worth it?"

Giving him no chance to reply, Anna drew in a long breath, inhaling the immortal magic from his body then, lifting her arms, hurled the malevolent god upwards.

Helpless, Odin was propelled towards the unforgiving stone ceiling of the cavern. He tried to fight the swift ascent, to no avail — Anna's power was too strong.

Odin crashed into the craggy roof. His neck snapped upon impact, and his body went limp. Anna forced him through the crevice, which shredded his flesh as he was ground against the jagged edges, and pitched him into the magma.

The fires of Earth consumed the once mighty god, instantly.

Anna watched the molten rock fill the hole left by Odin's body. A few drops of sizzling magma fell to the cavern floor, immediately solidifying into a single chunk of obsidian streaked with a rare and almost neon blue.

"Who's pitiful now?" she asked the fetid air pertly.

Bending, she picked up the stone, shoved it in her pocket, and ran to join her parents.

CHAPTER

ONE

I n the decade since Odin's demise at the hands of
Anna Helsdatter, life for the family had gained a sense
of normality.

Anna had watched her mother, Sela, grow into her
powers, thanks, in no small part, to the long-suffering —
and often amused — guidance of her father, Loki. Now, Sela
was able to control her magic without ending up in a
certain Dublin pub... although Sean and she *had* become
fast friends, swapping recipes whenever enthusiasm got
the better of her.

During the process, Sela had regained her passion to
lead but, heeding past mistakes, was no longer driven by
the desire to accumulate land and wealth.

Husband and wife had agreed to assume the roles of
Protectors of the Peace for all the Realms within Yggdrasil,
allowing the most powerful entity in existence to focus on
the more important trials with which someone her age had
to contend.

That of being a teenage girl, attending the local high
school, and getting embroiled in all the stuff, regular kids

seem to find irresistible. While this sounded good in theory, in practice, it did *not* necessarily equate to a smooth adolescence.

With parents who could, literally, pop in and out of their daughter's life, it was not uncommon for Sela to materialize when she sensed Anna was about to do something, she should not.

The primary example, and one which remained a bone of contention between Sela and Anna, occurred on the latter's first date, during her sophomore year in high school.

A boy on whom she had developed a serious crush, invited her to the movies. On the way home, they stopped, and perched on the hood of the boy's car to *gaze at the stars.*

When he decided to take the initiative and give Anna her first kiss, Sela appeared from nowhere and dragged her daughter home, after wiping the entire night from the boy's memory — of course.

The pair bickered for the rest of the evening and well into the early dawn. At length, Sela terminated the quarrel using the parental weapon, against which no child could argue... *Because I said so!*

In those moments, Anna sought refuge in one of two locations.

The first being the, supposedly, protective realm of her loving grandmother, Laufey. The ancient woman hid the child for extended periods and, with no daughter onto whom she could pass her wealth of knowledge, was happy to have an accomplice who shared her interest in potions, remedies, and recipes.

During these intervals and with wicked glee, Laufey divulged details of Loki's childhood, the good and the bad. Despite extracting Anna's promise that she would never use the information against her father, the escapades provided endless ammunition with which Anna could torment the god.

Anna justified forsaking her grandmother's trust by asking herself... *would Dad fail to take advantage of such juicy information?*

It was a truth Laufey could not deny, especially when she saw her son's mischievous twinkle in Anna's eyes.

The respite in this realm lasted until the day of a singularly acrimonious clash between Sela and Anna.

Unable to find her daughter in any of the normal haunts within Yggdrasil, to apologize for overreacting, Sela dared to check in the last place she should risk — Laufey's kitchen.

Readying herself for the anticipated physical assault associated with this domain, Sela was surprised — as were the two she was seeking — to discover that, imbued with Freya's magic, she no longer had to fear the time shift.

Relieved her daughter was safe in the care of her mother-in-law, Sela asked whether she might be of any help.

This led to Sundays at Grandma's for dinner.

Anna's other retreat was the adjacent house on the ranch, abode of Auntie Freya and Jacob. Already a second home when her parents were away on business, it became a bolt hole for Anna if things between mother and daughter were too terse for comfort.

Freya refused entry to Sela until tempers had cooled, and Anna had witnessed her aunt dousing the younger woman with a hose on more than one occasion, *suggesting* Sela go home until she got a grip.

Not that Anna escaped lightly. Freya had no hesitation in administering a verbal clip around the ear and, while she might offer her niece a haven, she did not take sides. "You two need to think before you speak," was her constant catch cry.

"Try listening to each other instead of blowing your tops. You never know, you might learn something." Freya's tolerant smile took the sting out of her admonishment and, skilled in the art of diversion, usually followed up any ticking off with a plea to help bake cookies or assist in some other household chore.

From deity to mortal, Freya had embraced the transition, and never regretted her decision to confer her considerable powers onto Sela, shouldering the role of — as Sela insisted on dubbing her — 'domestic goddess' with aplomb.

Anna was endlessly amazed at the ease with which Freya had adjusted to her change in status and, most especially, how her once vain aunt had accepted the aging process.

Despite wearing the Stetson, her husband had gifted her on their wedding night, the sun had bronzed her skin to a shade which belied her Nordic heritage. Anyone outside their circle, would be hard pressed to believe Freya was not reservation born and bred.

Her legendary blonde hair had blanched gracefully into beautiful white with attractive ash-gray highlights, and worn in a ponytail under the aforementioned Stetson when working the herds or, occasionally, a ballcap if she was visiting her cats in the mountains at the edge of the range.

That was *not* to say she had lost all her magic. Freya still had one or two tricks up her sleeve, which she used with alacrity, should circumstance demand. Neither had she any qualms about stepping in where angels... or gods... feared to tread... if there was no 'earthly' alternative.

In this same vein, it was Freya who raised a concerning question, one day when Anna was tending the garden with her aunt.

Taking a break, they sat atop the picnic table, sipping lemonade. Freya had been silent most of the afternoon, something Anna knew to be out of character. Freya's gaze was fixed on the horizon, but Anna could see something weighed on her mind.

"A silver penningar for your thoughts," Anna ventured.

"As if you could afford one of those with today's exchange rate, my dear." Freya laughed. "So let me give this one for free. Do you believe in reincarnation?"

"That's a heavy topic to discuss over a glass of lemonade, dontcha think?" Anna replied, trying to forestall this particular conversation.

Since her conception, Anna had wondered about her abilities; where they came from and how she had been able to reach out to Freya from the womb. The crux of the matter being that, if reincarnation was remotely possible, why were her memories confined to the beginning of *this* existence?

Freya paid no heed to Anna's attempt to deflect and, continuing to stare into the far distance, spoke her mind.

"There's something about you, something I feel I ought to recognise, yet I can't put my finger on it. As though we have met somewhere, or time, before. Even Jacob can't curb his curiosity over how quickly you took to hunting and the outdoor life. If you are from my past, reaching out to me from your mother's womb makes sense."

She studied her niece.

"Why didn't you talk to your mom instead of dragging me into it?"

Freya's swift change of subject brought a crooked smile to Anna's face. It relieved her of the necessity to contemplate a potentially checkered past, which may or may not have ended in an altercation with her favorite aunt.

The question Freya *had* posed was no less thought-provoking.

She recalled the time, she had tried to communicate with Sela, and the latter's unsatisfactory response.

Instead of her mother comprehending what Anna was desperate to convey, all she received was a *motherly* pat on her head when Sela stroked her pregnancy bump, and crooned what she had assumed to be a soothing, "It's okay, precious, settle down. I promise to lay off the deviled ham and ice cream until after you're born."

"Believe me, Auntie, I did, but Mom was so filled with pregnancy hormones, she thought what she was hearing was all in her mind."

Freya chuckled. "Yeah, Sela still has too many voices in her head."

Jumping down from the table, she held out her hand to Anna. "Enough philosophizing, those weeds aren't going to pick themselves."

"I could make them." Anna grinned hopefully, as she took the proffered hand and followed her aunt.

"And miss all this fresh air and exercise? Not a chance, deary. Now, get your butt a movin'. We still have half an acre to go."

"Ugh," Anna's instinctive response to anything undesirable. Such as being roped in to help Freya round up her recalcitrant felines.

The one-time charioteer of the cat-drawn carriage ensured her companions were not abandoned. At the beginning of winter, she brought the pair down to live in the house, despite Jacob's objection that Freya was mollycoddling the beasts.

The very definition of a rancher's wife, Freya ignored her husband.

For his part, Jacob had assumed the role of patriarch, although his ascension to that position remained a source of hilarity to the rest of his family, considering he was the youngest person on the property.

Jacob pointed out that Anna was definitely younger, to be reminded, only physically.

He had proven to be the perfect grandfather figure for Anna. Already her confidante throughout her life, it fell to him to have the *awkward* conversations with the teenager. To his chagrin, this had included the unavoidable one concerning sex.

Sela's efforts in that regard were an epic fail, given she had lost her virginity to a gang of marauders... whom she murdered... and was, subsequently, ensnared by Peer who used sex to enslave her.

It took Anna a long time to recover from the nightmares and psychological trauma, Sela's description of her horrific ordeal had triggered.

Assigning Loki that task was out of the question. The god could not be counted on to handle something of such a sensitive nature. The household was positive he would end up passing on secrets a fourteen-year-old should never know.

That left Jacob as the only one in whom Anna could trust.

One night, he sat her down and, after clarifying the mechanics of the act, explained how he had learned about love and sex the hard way, although not to the extent of Anna's mom, and that meeting and falling in love with Freya was the best thing ever to happen to him.

He left it that, assuring her, she would understand when it was her time, concluding with a grandfatherly warning.

"If I catch a boy trying to teach you what's what, I will beat him to death with a shovel and then bury his remains with what's left of it."

Anna rolled her eyes and giggled. She had no doubt of the old man's sincerity in issuing the threat.

Jacob, along with his brother, Uncle Randy, persevered with Anna's wilderness survival education. Inevitably, this led to her refereeing their sibling rivalry, which ranged from the correct method of setting a rabbit snare to baiting a fishing hook.

All in all, Anna appreciated the love and support she received growing up and, why — the day she packed up her VW Bug to head to college — was especially hard.

Unlike either her mother or aunt, Anna never saw cars as anything other than utilitarian. She could not fathom the fascination the older women in her life had for classic muscle cars. There was just enough room in Bug for everything she needed.

Excluding the furniture loaded into the back of Jacob's pickup... that stuff did not count.

CHAPTER
TWO

T
he decision to attend school at the University of South Dakota was not one her parents accepted readily.

With Anna's grade point average, and her participation in as many high school activities as she could manage, she was offered scholarships to such prominent universities as Stanford, Virginia, and Minnesota Law School.

Her choice of going to school in Vermillion was based on the small class size and the ability to undertake a double master's in law and history.

This morning's lecture made her question whether she had made the best choice.

Entering the second month of the semester, Anna had sparred academically with Professor Walter Simpson on more than a few occasions.

Considering most of Anna's immediate family predated human history, anything Simpson presented seemed painfully slanted to his own belief.

Unfortunately, he was her Academic Advisor, and she needed a decent grade in this class to graduate, as well as his approval of her topic for her major term paper, so she thought it wise to let him wallow in his personal propaganda.

Something Simpson did like a zealot.

The man took great pride in tracing his lineage, not only to a great aunt who had caused a monarchical crisis in England in the thirties, but also to a passenger on the Mayflower.

Said passenger, a certain Stephen Hopkins, was a man of whom most historians had a scurrilous opinion. Justly earned after committing such atrocities as participating in a mutiny which had endangered the lives of the survivors of a shipwreck who were stranded on a Caribbean Island for ten months.

It was only his knack of exploiting the pity of others which kept his neck out of a noose.

After the group built a boat and sailed to sanctuary, Hopkins returned to England, to ship himself and his new family to America.

Trouble followed him.

The man ran a tavern which served alcohol on Sundays — prohibited, sponsored shuffleboard contests, and flaunted the rules set down by the Mayflower Compact.

His previous experiences in the New World, and his ability to communicate with the local tribes people, meant most of his shady dealings were overlooked.

Here was where Simpson embellished Hopkins' importance; the very thing he had been prattling on about for the better part of class.

Bored, Anna elected to ignore his usual story time, preferring to read through the deluge of text messages she had received from her parents who were traveling around Asia on an extended holiday.

Eventually, Simpson noticed the inattention of his star pupil.

Attempting to drag Anna back into the discussion, he invited, "Ms. Helsdatter. Perhaps you can enlighten your classmates as to who should be credited with discovering the New World?"

Shifting her gaze from her phone to the shoddily dressed professor at the front of the room, a wicked smile curved Anna's lips, and she thought it time to teach *him* a lesson in the process.

Drawing a breath, she plunged headlong into a dissertation which might have earned the average student their master's degree.

"To answer that question would require an understanding of the varying perspectives regarding this *discovery*.

"If it were yours, Professor Simpson, I'd suppose you to be fixated on Columbus, though I dare say you would be happier if you were able to link him to your infamous, excuse me, famous ancestor."

Anna's snide shot prompted a round of muted chuckles.

"Ms. Helsdatter," Simpson started, but Anna was much like Sela in that, once wound up, there was no stopping her.

"Were you to ask my immediate family, it would be Leif Eriksson. On the other hand, according to my grandpa, the continent should be described, more accurately, as 'previously unencountered', until such time as it was *appropriated* by your ancestors following an armed invasion.

"Of course, let's not forget the Chinese landing in South America, or the Polynesians in California.

"Maybe you prefer my Uncle Sean's theory that it was one of his ancestor's, Saint Brendan the Navigator, although I'm not sure how a Catholic priest, let alone an

Irish saint, could leave a direct line of descendants. I guess that's a topic for the Seminarians in Sioux Falls to ponder."

Her observation elicited a second bout of mirth, no longer quite so subtle.

"Ms. Helsdatter, if you would please—"

"Oh, you are correct, Professor, how could I possibly forget the Egyptians, or the Phoenicians, or at the very least, according to the guy on TV with the crazy hair, Ancient Aliens from outer space."

The room erupted in howls of laughter.

Simpson lost his cool and slammed his hands on his desk.

"Ms. Helsdatter, see me in my office immediately after class."

Keenly aware she was going to receive a disciplinary rebuke, Anna was still a Helsdatter and the offspring of Loki and, as such could not prevent herself from adding, "May I ask why? Did I miss somebody? Perhaps the Virgin Mary, *with* the Holy Grail?"

"Out. *Now.*"

Although Anna saved her blatant disrespect for Professor Simpson, her other lecturers were not spared, should they insist on teaching their opinion and not the facts.

She had found a quiet corner in the Student Union and while preparing for her next class, a tutorial, had collated a litany of source evidence from the material she was reading, on the off-chance Dr. Nichols decided to pull a 'Simpson' on them.

A glance at her watch told her Simpson's lecture was over, but she had no intention of enduring another about his disapproval of her attitude. She had heard enough of it already.

"You'll never get anywhere if you don't knuckle down and follow the rules," his tedious rhetoric rang in her brain.

Simpson's annoying voice was replaced with an amused and far more welcome one.

"You know, my sweet little sister, you really ought to stop causing problems for yourself."

Her brother's gentle chiding eased her mood. With a sigh, she defended, "Jörmungandr, you have no idea what a complete twat the man is."

The step-siblings had long since established their own psychic pathway of communicating. They could reach each other at will, especially if one of them was feeling down.

Their conversations usually involved the younger sister catching her older brother up on current affairs, and teaching him slang.

Jörmungandr chuckled. "Ahh, but was it not you who said everyone on Earth is here for a reason?"

"Well, his must be to drive me insane, and stop using my words against me."

"Then stop giving me reasons."

They both laughed.

Anna loved her brother and, although she wished there was a way to free him of his confinement, accepted he held a special purpose in the world.

Frequent visits had helped Anna come to terms with her brother's situation. Jörmungandr knew he was not alone, and demonstrated his appreciation with a subtlety unexpected from so huge a creature, becoming Anna's sounding board, mediator, and moral compass.

"Hey, Jö." A diminutive only she used. "Can you do me a favor and keep this between the two of us? You know how Mom and Dad worry."

"Is that Helsdatter speak for being lectured?"

Anna sensed her brother's wry grin. "You know what I mean, just promise me."

"Only if you promise to come see me."

"Already have you scribbled in for my next holiday. Right between getting my nails done and shopping for new shoes."

"Gee, I am honored."

"You should be. My time is precious. I don't give it to—"

An unexpected quiver shook the building. In a place where tremors over 3 rarely occurred, this one was enough to rattle coffee cups on the counter, sending a barista screaming for cover.

"Knock it off, ya bully. I was just kidding," Anna ordered.

"Then don't get too big for your britches, kiddo."

"Yeah, yeah," she grumbled. "See you at Thanksgiving."

"Deal."

Her brother's presence fading from her mind, Anna resumed her reading assignment. Confident in her abilities, she convinced herself, *I should have just enough time to finish before class.*

Screech.

The sound of a chair being dragged across the tiled floor, reminiscent of nails along a blackboard, set Anna's teeth on edge.

Growling inwardly, she glared at its new occupant.

Puffed up like a turkey, her Resident Assistant, Renner McDaniels. While she had a cordial relationship with the guy, she also tried to avoid him like the plague.

Unfortunately, Renner could not take a hint and used any pretext to seek her out.

"Good afternoon, Anna," Renner chirped with a cheesy grin. "Shouldn't you be in class right now? I know Simpson frowns on his students skipping."

While Anna's fellow female students might find his acquaintance with their schedules, unsettling, Anna was not most people.

"Let's just say we had a difference of historical opinion. If there's nothing you need, Renner, I have to finish this chapter."

"Oh, but there is. How would you like to be the lucky girl to accompany me for beer and pizza at the Pub tonight?"

Anna failed to conceal the scoff, "Let me guess, my treat?"

Renner feigned affront. "You cut me to the quick, Ms. Helsdatter."

"Don't tempt me, Renner. Besides, I have a ton of research to do for my paper, so, sadly, I shall have to decline."

"Not even if I throw in a couple of tickets to a movie of your choice."

"Nope, I prefer to stream them in my room, than get my feet stuck on the gross floor of a theater."

"Great idea. How about I stop by your quad with said beer and pizza? We could stream on *Nutflex*. I guarantee you'd be begging for a sequel."

Anna laughed off his self-invitation. "Mr. McDaniels, *I* would suggest you excuse yourself before I stomp on your *subscription*, canceling it permanently."

The feet of the chair scraped hesitantly as Renner stood, his face betraying nothing of his uncertainty regarding her capacity to harm his manhood. He inclined his head. "Please, reconsider. It would definitely be... advantageous."

She watched Renner leave, then heard the recently vacated chair whine again.

Huffing, she turned to find Simpson's Teaching Assistant, Shelly Connelly, staring over her shoulder at the retreating McDaniels.

Swiveling to face Anna, Shelly asked, "How long have you and Renner been a thing?"

Anna snorted, "I'm thinking every night in his dreams."

Shelly made a gagging noise. "I'd recommend staying away from him, hon. He might be a mighty benchwarmer for the Coyote's football team, but he spends all his free time sniffing around the first years."

"Wow, I didn't realize you were so well informed about campus life."

"I'm serious. There's even a joke going around that he should transfer to SDSU and be their college mascot. The word is, he screws around like a jackrabbit and crosses the finish line faster than one."

"Okay, Shelly... ewwww... and, changing the topic before I hurl, what brings my prof's overworked and under-appreciated TA to my table. Is your master sending you into the general population to search me out?"

"Hardly, he's still storming around his office, waving his copy of Dante's *Inferno* like he's trying to summon Satan and have you banished to the Sixth Circle. The man believes every word out of your mouth is nothing but heresy. Though, he's not sure whether the eighth or ninth level wouldn't suit you better."

"Fraud and Treachery? Cute. If he wants to send me anywhere, how about somewhere that actually exists, so I can see my family?"

Shelly sent Anna a queer look, "Huh?"

"Never mind. That doesn't explain your presence."

"Just promise me to take it easy on him," Shelly cajoled, "I can't afford to lose this gig if you do manage to give him apoplexy."

"Fine. Tell him you did your due diligence, reprimanded me appropriately, and I swore to be a good student from now on."

"As if he'd believe that. How about I go with, we talked and you'll try not to disrupt class anymore."

"If you think he'll believe that lie any better, go for it."

"Thanks, doll," Shelly said with a slow smile. "Oh, and don't forget your outline is due on his desk by Monday."

"I'll hand it in as soon as I can. That is if peeps would leave me alone long enough to finish."

Shelly giggled, patting Anna's hand as she left the younger student to her work.

THREE

S hrugging into a voluminous, garishly striped robe, Anna gathered a couple of towels thinking that it was at times like this, she wished she had stayed on the ranch.

Even after adjusting to the social aspects of interpersonal interaction during high school, living cheek by jowl with people who were, basically, strangers still made her uncomfortable and, being a neat freak, was *not* a fan of sharing a bathroom.

Closing the door, she tossed her towels over the rail, and hung her robe on one of the hooks screwed into the wall.

Standing in front of the mirror, she poked and prodded her naked body, certain she was falling victim to the Freshman Fifteen weight gain.

Comparing herself with her mother's athletic physique and her aunt's fabled beauty whenever she studied her reflection, she found herself wanting.

Tonight was no exception.

"More like Freshman Twenty," Anna groused at the

mirror, even though her reflection desperately tried to convince her it was all in her head.

She could hear her grandfather's exasperation on the subject. "Geez, youngsters these days, always moaning about their weight. If you're that worried, couple days yoked to a plow'll sort ya."

Anna chuckled softly. "Thanks, Jacob."

Relieved she had not been assigned to a forward-thinking dorm building where the opposite sexes — all fifty-seven varieties officially recognized by Admissions — shared a common bathroom and shower facility, her quad still meant she had to put up with three other people — none of whom seemed capable of grasping the concept of privacy... or modesty.

She came to believe the phrase, 'born in a barn' originated in South Dakota.

It had taken Anna the better part of a month to persuade two of the girls, Brooke and Kendra, who were smitten with each other at first sight, to close their bedroom door when they felt like exploring their sexuality.

Her third roommate, Zoe, spent little time in the quad but when she did, adding insult to injury, her annoying boyfriend was in tow.

If Anna had to imagine what a bordello was like, all she had to do was listen to the sounds emanating from Zoe's room. Needless to say, Anna preferred her absence.

A state of affairs which worked in Myst's favor. Zoe's usually deserted room offered the perfect concealment, as she plotted to wreak vengeance against a certain college first year and her family.

The valkyrie had stalked Anna since the day she had learned of Odin's unjust demise. Myst had served the All Father without question for the entirety of her existence. Anything he asked of her, she did willingly.

That included stripping any other deity who stepped into Odin's Hall of their unique powers, which were restored the moment each departed. The brief loss, never detected.

While Myst considered Anna, because of her youth, to be the weakest member of her family, she also sensed an indefinable potency radiating from the girl. Unable to attribute such formidable magic to a mere child, Myst surmised it originated from the strange charm Anna wore around her neck.

Doubtless conjured up by that witch, Freya, Myst had reasoned.

Everything about the pendant seemed to mock the valkyrie, especially the unusual streak, bright in the onyx-coloured stone, which recalled the azure hue of Odin's eye — a feature she loved and missed.

If the opportunity presented itself, Myst pledged to

destroy it as well. *Mayhap, I'll use the chain to strangle the girl first.*

Before Anna started college, Myst had to maintain a safe distance from her target. Those who surrounded Anna during her adolescence never wandered far from her.

What was the term humans used for that type of child rearing? Myst mused frequently. *Helicopter Parenting? Nay, more like Prison Guarding.*

On the upside, this meant no one in the quaint family had any idea of the fate awaiting them.

The dorm proved a greater test of her ingenuity, but Myst had discovered, by loitering in Zoe's room, she could keep track of Anna. Of late, bereft of the augmented powers Odin had bestowed on her in Valhalla combined with Zoe's unannounced appearances, the valkyrie struggled to sustain her concealment.

It had reached the point that when the room was empty, which, owing to midterms had grown few and far between, an exhausted Myst manifested and collapsed on Zoe's bed.

A detestable predicament, not only because of the risk of being discovered, but also, the lingering aroma of sex which clung to the sheets.

Bad enough, she had to suffer being a voyeur to the couple's seemingly insatiable lust, and although not naive to the perverse sexual proclivity with which Odin and the other deities in Valhalla chose to pursue each other, to be reminded of it with each breath was intolerable.

What these humans consider to be an emotional joining was something an ethereal, such as myself, should never be forced to experience.

Sadly, beggars can't be choosers.

The sound of Anna closing the door when she entered the quad stirred Myst from a fitful slumber. The overwhelming surge of energy pulsing through the walls caused Myst to scramble off Zoe's bed and meld into the furthest corner of the girl's room before Anna became conscious of her.

Fearful, she had not disguised her presence in time, Myst held her breath and waited for her foe to burst through the door intent on confronting the valkyrie.

No one came.

Instead, she heard Anna complaining about the state of the common area and the inability of anyone to keep the bathroom door shut. Moments later, she heard water running on the other side of one wall.

Edging her way out of the bedroom, sure she would be discovered — if only by the smell of the couple's pheromones which seemed impregnated on every surface — Myst crept to the closed bathroom door.

The valkyrie wrinkled her pert nose in confusion. Conscious of the immense power exuding from her hated enemy, Myst sensed a subtle, almost indefinable difference, as though Anna had somehow isolated an element of her magic.

About to dismiss such arrant nonsense... *why separate your powers, and why choose to?*... Myst paused, recalling her belief the girl's power was not inherent. A sly smile slid across her face, gratified her assumption was correct.

The smile faltered.

Startled, Myst registered that the disparate essence she

had deciphered, carried a wisp of familiarity, like the memory of a long-departed lover's gentle caress.

Odin?

The magic which beckoned did not come from the bathroom. Its source was Anna's bedroom.

Ignoring her target for the moment, Myst tiptoed into the room. Her eyes widened when she caught sight of the pendant dangling from the edge of a mirror.

Her heart drummed wildly in her chest, and she swore she heard Odin plead from within the stone, "Please, my faithful child. Please free me from my prison."

Trembling, she let down her guard, her ghost-like form becoming incarnate so she could retrieve the accursed gem.

Inches from her prize, Myst heard the lock on the quad's front door click.

Expecting the new arrival to be one of Anna's roommates, Myst peered out of the bedroom, perplexed to see a male shutting the door with quiet stealth.

What do we have here? A burglar? Her lip curled disdainfully. Unlike any burglar, she had seen, he wore no mask, and she doubted thieves carried keys.

With neither time to waste, nor a plausible excuse for being in Anna's room, Myst melted into the shadows which darkened the far corner.

From her vantage point, she had a reasonable view through the half-closed bedroom door, and recognized the man who paid the odd visit to the quad, on the pretense of dorm business. Typically, this included alleged complaints from their neighbors about the various comings and goings of the four, and how they ought to behave themselves lest he be required to punish them.

Every time he left, they griped about what a creep he was and how uncomfortable he made them feel.

That was their problem.

Curious now, Myst watched him hesitate by the bathroom door. The lascivious look on his face, as he listened to Anna sing while she showered, made Myst's stomach roil.

His attention shifted to Anna's bedroom.

The valkyrie held her breath.

D-Did he hear me?

Watching him approach, Myst prepared to spring into action.

Another quick glance at the bathroom, and he slipped into Anna's room.

To Myst's surprise, the male stopped at Anna's dressing table where the pendant hung.

She canted her head as he ran his fingers along the slender gold chain, until the polished fragment of obsidian rested in the palm of his hand. Clutching it in his fist, he yanked it from its perch.

Naught but a lowlife thief, Myst sneered inwardly.

She saw him check the closed bathroom door again, then hurry past it to exit the quad, careful to make no sound.

Angry at losing the stone and perplexed as to why the wretch had stolen it, Myst followed him.

The hair on her nape prickled when she heard the bathroom door fling open and Anna yell, "Who's here? Kendra, if that's you, I'm gonna kick your ass for using all my bodywash... *again*.

Myst vanished before Anna could identify the intruder.

In the safe confines of the crowded hallway, Myst emerged from the shadows. Fortunately for her, the students who called this floor home were too busy with their own lives to notice another female blinking into existence in the corridor.

Myst paid them no heed; her gaze fixed on the male heading to the staircase.

Allowing him to get ahead, but not far enough to lose sight of him, Myst pursued him down the stairs.

When the male reached the first-floor door, he made sure no one was chasing him, barely missing Myst becoming one with the wall.

Preoccupied by the object of his petty crime, one of many throughout his life, it was doubtful he would have noticed her anyway. He suspected this rock held a higher value than any decrepit ten-speed bike or battered game console, he might have purloined previously.

What he had done was risky, not to mention poorly executed but, if he wanted to impress the object of his fantasies, turning this tawdry trinket into a glittering ring would surely win her approval and, subsequently, her heart.

"What girl could turn down such a romantic gesture." He chuckled to himself. "Don Juan has nothing on me."

Shoving the stone into his pocket, he shouldered open the door leading to his corridor, letting it swing closed behind him.

Keeping her distance, Myst watched him unlock a vivid red door. Like its tenant, the color screamed out its arrogance among the standard white-painted pine entryways.

"Who would expect anything less?" Myst muttered as she followed.

Halting in front of it, she studied the badly applied

gloss, considering her next move. Even before her eyes focused on the occupant card, Myst knew the name — Renner McDaniels, Residential Assistant.

Conjuring up a realistic river of human tears, Myst pounded against the RA's door, frantically.

"Please, please, help me. I've lost my keys and I'm locked out of my dorm."

Beating the wood with tiny but fierce fists, she began to worry she might punch a hole in the panelling by accident.

Thankfully, before that occurred, Renner poked his head out, barking, "Jesus Christ. Are you trying to raise the..." The remainder of the question froze in his throat as the most beautiful co-ed stood before him, in hysterics.

Females like this were the very reason Renner had become an RA. They usually offered little resistance as he soothed them into his bed.

Guys like Renner were the easiest for Myst to glamor. She played on their fantasies of the perfect woman and, while not the prettiest of the valkyries, neither was she the homeliest. That honor had belonged to her long-departed sister, Róta.

Sniveling pitifully, Myst appeared to be the epitome of a damsel in distress.

Inwardly gloating, Renner, assumed a solicitous expression. "Come in, come in. I'm sure we can get this sorted."

CHAPTER
FOUR

Myst stepped over the threshold into a world defined by narcissism to a degree which rivaled Odin.

Instead of walls adorned with trophies displaying the All Father's hunting prowess, the accolades here were unalloyed vanity.

The pictures, which looked to be arranged meticulously, depicted Renner clad in various sporting attire or, and with disturbing predominance, exposing more flesh than anyone with a modicum of decency would exhibit.

"Sit down and tell me what's going on," Renner invited graciously, escorting Myst to his shabby couch.

Myst repeated her plea, "I was in the process of moving in and my door..."

"Moving in?" Renner repeated. "Nobody told me about a new transfer," suspicion cooling his tone.

"I-I don't know about that," Myst hedged. "All I know is Admissions assigned me a room on the third floor."

"Just like them," he grumbled. "Nobody tells me anything until shit happens."

"Oh, please... I'm so sorry to cause you problems," she replied demurely. "I'll just go over to Admin—"

"No," Renner countered in no uncertain terms, his brusque attitude taking Myst by surprise. Only Odin had ever addressed her in so curt a manner.

"Ex-excuse me?" In high dudgeon, she contemplated smiting the impertinent mortal.

"Forgive me," Renner apologized with practiced contrition. "I shouldn't take out my annoyance with the faculty on you. Now, you said you were locked out of your room. Which one was it?"

Myst had not considered the answer to this question, and blurted out, "Third floor, three-twenty."

Her response elicited a queer arching of Renner's brow. "You sure about that? I thought that one was filled already, but with those numb nits in Admin, who knows."

Casually, Renner moved to his makeshift bar — in actuality, a sheet of plywood balanced on four stacks of bricks.

His back to Myst, Renner splashed shots of assorted spirits into a tumbler, adding one last key ingredient to the concoction before screwing the lid on tightly, and shaking it vigorously.

"I know alcohol for Freshmen is against the rules, but it's gonna take me a bit to find the replacement keys and you look like you could use something to calm you."

While Renner was busy bartending, Myst noticed something poking out from underneath a magazine... the cover of which featured a nude female whose pose left nothing to the imagination... tossed carelessly onto the piecemeal coffee table.

Nudging the trashy magazine aside, she came face to face with four photographs of scantily clad college co-eds, spread-eagled on the same couch she was sitting on; all passed out.

Glaring at the sleaze across the room, she watched him pour whatever he had brewed into a semi-clean glass.

She hid the pictures before he returned to where she sat.

With what he believed was a saccharine smile, Renner said, "Bottoms up cutie, I'll be right back."

A judicious sniff informed Myst, she would be wise not to drink anything this man gave her. She put the glass on the coffee table, and waited until he was focused on searching for the appropriate key amongst the mishmash of other spare keys in a wall cabinet.

With an infinitesimal disturbance of air, she reappeared behind him, whispering into his ear before he realized she had moved, "Tsk, I surmised you were a disgusting human who uses his position to steal from women, but I did not deem you repellent enough to resort to drugging one in order to satisfy yourself."

Renner froze, and his voice shook as he tried to dismiss the accusations, "I-I have n-no idea what you are talking about."

Slender fingers reached into his pocket to snag the chain. His gaze dropped to the strange gemstone dangling from his guest's grasp.

"Come now, Renner, lying sullies your image even more," Myst added silently, *if that was in any way possible.*

Renner's throat was parched as he forced a reply, unable to fathom how this bitch knew so much about him, never mind that she had figured out his specialty drink.

He scoured his brain for an explanation which portrayed him as the romantic hero not the villain. His plan to take the necklace to a backstreet jeweler, he knew, to have the stupid stone cut into smaller pieces then transformed into a beautiful ring — one so impressive, there would be no way Anna could refuse him — might not pass muster.

Too late, this stranger could expose him as a thief and rapist.

He was not looking at probation or expulsion. He was looking at jail time. Hard time at that.

Scrabbling to concoct a credible story, Renner felt the warmth of his visitor's breath against his ear once more, her words curling inwards, teasing his mind. As though the Devil himself was offering an escape clause.

"Perhaps there is a way out of this predicament, you find yourself in. Do you desire more power than any mere human?"

Slowly, Renner pivoted to face Myst, swallowing hard when he saw her semi-translucent state. He blinked rapidly, trying to clear his vision, suspecting he was suffering from an aneurysm.

Myst reassured, "I possess magic you cannot comprehend. Anything I promise, I can fulfil."

"A-are you some sort of demon?" Renner stammered stupidly.

"Well, boy, that depends on your answer. Are you willing to assume the imperium of a god? Not just any deity, like that fool Loki, I offer you the wisdom and strength of the All Father, himself."

"W-what the hell are you going on about? Assume the imperium of a god? Wait, did I get drunk, and fall asleep watching a Thor movie? That makes sense. Except, now I'm talking to myself." Renner's forehead creased in confusion.

Myst blew an exasperated sigh. "Look closely at the

stone on this infernal necklace. Do you see the vein running through it?

His initial fear dwindling, and presuming this was a dream, Renner jeered, "Yeah, yeah, it's bright blue. So what?"

"Not close enough, ignoramus." Myst fisted the chain, and rammed the gem through the bridge of Renner's nose, shattering the stone. Shards pierced his skull, and a chunk sank into the dying man's right eye, destroying it.

Myst stepped back as the human crumpled to the ground. Fascinated, she bent over to watch him expire.

In the numerous clashes she had fought in Odin's name, Myst never lingered near the fallen long enough to witness the spirit crossing over to whatever eternity its host had believed in.

Today was different and she was held immobile, noting Renner's gaze did not grow cloudy.

As he passed from one realm to another, the dull indigo of the remaining eye began to brighten, morphing into the distinct glacial blue of a far more esteemed owner.

As Renner's body released its original occupant's soul, another took its place. The eye which had transfixed Myst, dilated and winked its consciousness at her.

Myst dropped to one knee and bowed her head. "Are you well, All Father?"

Slowly, Odin rose to his feet as, instinctively, his fingers touched his empty eye socket. A disgruntled grimace contorted his features. "Even now, Mímir, you hold me to your bloody payment for knowledge... "

Odin paused, the day he sacrificed an eye to gain invaluable insight rearing up in his mind. The scowl softened slightly as he recalled taking counsel from a disembodied head.

"...a sip of your wisdom water would serve me well right now, old friend," his acerbic tone turned pensive.

In a whisper, Myst confessed, "I beg forgiveness, Odin. It was my negligence which caused the loss of your beautiful eye. I was too impetuous in requisitioning the human's body for you."

"Silence," he commanded, shedding the unwelcome nostalgia. "We shall consider your punishment another day. For now..." Odin stretched and twisted as though trying Renner's body on like a new suit of armor. "...you might have put better effort into searching for a replacement shell."

"All Father, this one has access to places others do not and, from my observations, no one cares about him."

About to reiterate his disdain, Odin was interrupted by somebody pounding on the door.

The pair fell silent but, instead of abating, the banging escalated.

Odin perceived who was in the hallway before the visitor spoke.

"Renner, I know you're in there. I can smell your sickening cologne from here. I need to report a theft from my room."

Myst headed to the door, determined to end the pursuit once and for all. With Odin by her side, it would be a short battle.

As she reached out to grasp the doorknob, Odin stopped her.

"Are you insane?" he snarled under his breath.

"This is our chance to rid the world of her before we destroy her family," Myst contested. "I realize you have just regained your strength, Master, but she is only a pathetic human."

"Who do you think entrapped me?"

The door was rattling in the frame as Anna's anger at Renner's lack of response increased.

"Surely, it was Loki," Myst contended.

"Hardly, it was the monster on the other side of that door. Can you not feel her power intensifying with each second?"

"I-is not that y-your strength?"

"I could only sacrifice to the heavens to reach her capability. Now vanish, so I can deal with her."

Doing as Odin bade, Myst camouflaged herself behind the bar.

Remembering his missing eye, Odin grabbed a towel to cover it and, taking a breath, cast a concealment spell to mask his burgeoning power. Despite being confined in the stone for so long, he was confident it was robust enough to prevent his immortal enemy from discovering the truth.

Unlocking the door, he swung it open. Standing face-to-face with the bitch responsible for the loss of everything he held dear, Odin wanted nothing more than to eliminate her.

It is not the time.

Swallowing the bile clawing at his throat, he asked, "What the hell is your grief?"

Inhabiting Renner's body had granted Odin access to the cur's thoughts and attitude, along with the titillating detail that Renner was infatuated with Anna. Knowledge he could use to his advantage.

Being rude will trigger suspicion, he told himself. *Be smart.*

"Geez." Anna flinched. "Did I interrupt you pleasuring yourself or something?"

"Sorry, Anna. It's been a hard day."

"Apparently. Did somebody finally punch you in the eye?"

"Nothing so dramatic, just an infection. Wanna see?" Odin leaned closer.

"Ewww, hardly. Last thing I need is a communicable disease from you."

Odin crossed to the bar and, without relinquishing the towel, poured himself something from a bottle declaring itself to be Kentucky Bourbon. The smoky flavour with an underlying sweetness was surprisingly palatable.

He savoured the spirit, letting it slide down his throat. *Ahhhh…* he had missed the taste of alcohol during the decade of his imprisonment.

"Would you care for one," he offered politely.

"No, I want you to do your job. Somebody broke into my dorm and stole my pendant, while I was showering for crying out loud. Whoever took it might well have assaulted me if I'd come out of the bathroom at the wrong time. Here am I believing this campus is supposed to be safe."

Taking a sip of the spirit, Odin retorted into the glass, "Highly doubtful."

"What did you say?" Anna snapped, unsure whether he was being snide.

"I said I doubt they've pawned it yet. I'll contact campus police and have them search the dorms."

"You really are as useless as they come, Renner."

"Not much more I can do for you, Anna. I'm an RA, not a cop."

"Yeah, you'd love a pair of handcuffs wouldn't you." Anna taunted, and stalked off, slamming the door behind her.

She heard Renner say as the door banged into the frame, "Thanks for stopping by. Drop in anytime."

CHAPTER
FIVE

Returning to the quad, Anna was startled to see her mother in the common area, chatting breezily with Zoe over a coffee.

"...and you'd be so proud of our Anna. She aced her midterms. I hate her for it," Zoe confided, and both women chuckled at the statement, which was only partially a joke.

The soft click of the door snagged their attention.

In her hurry to get to Renner's room after discovering the theft, Anna, remembering to get dressed — if one could call the baggy T and crumpled shorts, dressed — had forgotten her hair was still wrapped in a towel.

Zoe trilled, "Hey, hon. Look who I found wandering our corridor."

Sela tsk'ed at her daughter standing on the threshold, agape, her face warming into an amused smile as she turned back to Zoe, "She had the same look on her face when I found her in a car with some boy from high school."

"Mom," Anna implored, hoping to prevent her mother from recounting that horrible memory.

Zoe giggled, and rose from her chair to leave mother

and daughter together. Before she passed Anna in the doorway, Zoe reminded Sela, "Don't forget, Mrs. Helsdatter—"

"Please, Zoe, call me Sela. All my friends and enemies do."

Zoe put her hand on Anna's shoulder. "I love her."

"Try living with her. I think you'd change your mind."

Waving off Anna's opinion, Zoe repeated, "Don't forget, *Sela,* tonight is taco and margarita night, and you promised to join us.

"Okay, catch you later."

Zoe paused long enough to inform Anna, "Oh, and I volunteered you to be on cleanup duty. Later."

Shaking her head wearily at this parting shot, Anna closed the door behind her, and plopped into the chair Zoe had vacated. "May I ask why I have the pleasure of your presence, besides to charm my roommate?"

"Is that any way to greet your concerned parent?" Sela replied, a note of hurt in her voice.

"I'm sorry, Mom. It's been a long day, and to top things off, someone—"

"Stole your pendant? I already sensed that, and the reason I'm here. How many times have I told you to get rid of that damned necklace."

"I know, I screwed up, but there was no way to dispose of it safely."

"And now someone else has it. Someone who has *no* idea what will happen if they damage that stone—"

Sela stopped mid-sentence. Her face paled. It was as though Hel's long-dead, cold hand had reached out from the grave to stroke her icy fingers down Sela's spine.

Her dread-laden gaze shifted to Anna.

Vapor escaped Anna's lips as the chill hit her, and she nodded. "Yeah, I feel it, too. Is Dad around?"

Sela shook her head. "No, that's not his aura. Besides, I sent him to the ranch the moment we felt the world tilt."

She recalled the look on her husband's face when she dispatched him back to Montana, just in case protection was needed there. It had reminded her of the night in Manhattan when they were forced to flee the warmth of their home.

To convince Anna her father had agreed willingly, Sela offered, "He grumbled something about keeping himself busy brewing mead until I get back."

"What? Mom, are you crazy? You left Dad alone with a batch of freshly brewed alcohol?"

"Who do you think you're talking to, daughter? Of course, I didn't. I asked Freya and Jacob to watch over him."

"So, you're telling me all three of them are drunk off their asses? Please, Mom, go home and warn them Odin's been freed."

"If you think I'm gonna leave you to face that bastard on your own, you're crazier than your father. Besides, if two deities can't handle that old man, I'm sure Jacob will be more than happy to introduce Odin to his trench gun."

"I doubt that would do any good."

"Might not kill him, but the buckshot Jacob loads in that shotgun would deter Odin from trying anything stupid."

"There's nothing I can say that will make you change your mind?" Anna begged her mother to reconsider.

"None whatsoever."

"And where do you plan to sleep?"

Sela eyed the couch.

"Oh, no you don't. There's already enough potential victims in this quad," Anna chided, hoping this would discourage her mother from staying; she didn't need anyone else to worry about.

"Too late, Zoe already said it was okay," Sela replied smugly. "I'm sure she'd be upset if you sent your poor old mother to sleep in some dingy roadside inn."

"This, from the woman who used to sleep on blood-soaked battlefields, not to mention Helheim. Don't try to kick me out of my bed if you get a stiff back from the couch. Remember, it was a hand-me-down from the previous tenants.

"I try to avoid sitting on it altogether. I hate to imagine what happened on it."

Tapping her index finger on her chin, Anna gave it one last try. "Sure you don't want to stay in a motel?"

Zoe returned to the dorm after sunset, the promised tacos, but not — to Anna's delight — her boyfriend, in tow.

About an hour later, Brooke and Kendra came in, and fell on what remained of the meal, although Kendra did feel moved to complain about the lack of nachos.

"Not my fault, I told you not to be late. Order some more if you want them that badly." Zoe glared.

Flipping Zoe the bird, Kendra rooted about the kitchen for chips and dip, grumbling about greedy roommates. Wisely, Brooke stayed out of it, opting to pour the drinks.

Eventually, aided by several glasses of wine, peace reigned, and the group settled down to watch a movie.

It was close to midnight when Anna who was fighting to keep her eyes open, dragged herself off the sofa to wash the empty glasses. Leaving them to drain, she excused herself, bidding her mother and roommates a goodnight, grinning at the drowsy responses.

Sitting on the edge of her bed, she touched her throat where her chain usually hung, then glanced at the mirror where she had left it earlier.

Shutting her eyes, she tried to trace its whereabouts, but came up blank. In despair, Anna buried her face in her hands.

"How do I protect my family now?" she beseeched the Fates, who did not deign to respond.

Tired of trying, Anna curled up under the covers, and drifted off to sleep.

Anna's eyes fluttered open. She stared, blinked, shook her head, and stared again, not quite believing what she was seeing.

Spread out in front of her, a winter wonderland... yet, she did not feel cold. A frown creased her brow. The landscape was harsh but breathtakingly beautiful and, curiously, it felt like home.

What the hell was going on?

She tried to get her bearings, a series of images flitting through her head, accompanied by myriad emotions... grief, fury, enmity, resignation, acquiescence... almost too fast for comprehension.

"Enough," she yelled to the vast emptiness. "Where am I?"

"This is your beginning," a vaguely familiar voice

echoed across the stillness. "I deemed it essential you understand your... origins."

"And you are?"

There was a lengthy pause.

Anna was on the verge of giving vent to an infuriated scream when she heard, "One whom you should trust."

Recalling her mother's tales of her time in purgatory, banished there by someone she *trusted,* Anna's lip curled contemptuously. "That remains to be seen."

A low chuckle reached her. "Listen and learn," came the confident reply.

The pictures coalesced to create a timeline of sorts, as the spectral voice gave a running commentary.

"You walked the northlands as Skadi, a jötunn and daughter of Thiazi, your true father who, after kidnapping Idunn, the goddess of immortality was killed by the trickster, Loki."

About to issue a strenuous denial that her father, in this existence, was capable of murder, Anna held her tongue.

In truth Loki was, as were all the gods, guilty of numerous questionable, if not downright criminal offenses. Also, she discerned something in the tone of the voice, a sly note which suggested obfuscation.

The offspring of two deities, Anna had made it her business to study Norse mythology.

Forewarned is forearmed was her mantra.

She waited.

"You sought to avenge Thiazi's untimely demise and, donning battle gear, stormed Asgard. We averted your wrath by offering you a husband from among the gods..."

From the swirling darkness of long-forgotten memory, the image of a rich red curtain from under which poked a row of sandaled feet, formed in Anna's mind.

She suppressed an irreverent giggle, aware this was no laughing matter.

"Seems this Skadi chick was not particularly upset about her father's death," Anna sniped. "A husband seems a rather pathetic recompense."

"Do not interrupt," the speaker sounded impatient. "You chose Njord, God of the Sea, but your union was doomed. Everything you touch is doomed," the voice had taken on a discordance which jarred Anna's ears.

"And the reason you felt it essential to apprise me of this... legend?" Anna asked, with forced politeness, still trying to decide whether this was a dream or she had been sucked into some weird time shift.

When it came to the gods, nothing surprised her.

"To be in possession of the facts provides a clearer picture, revealing that what you have been told and what is the truth are not one and the same. That your unconditional trust in certain people is grossly misplaced."

"In whom ought I to place my trust?" Anna parried innocently.

"One who can save you," the voice seemed to be fading.

"*Save* me? From what?"

"Those who seek to arrest your powers."

Anna strained to hear the words which were carried away on the wind. The snow at her feet whipped up to swirl around her in a writhing vortex, and she fought to free herself from the suffocating whiteness...

"Anna, *Anna*, wake up, you're having a nightmare. **Anna**."

The soft caress of a cool hand on her cheek and the calm coaxing, penetrated Anna's panic, and she bolted upright, gasping for breath. Her wild gaze met the unruffled one of her mother.

"Mom." Anna shuddered, and for the first time in over a decade, burst into tears, clinging to Sela for dear life.

"Hey, it's okay, sweetheart. You're safe, I'm here."

Sela rocked her daughter as she had when Anna was a babe, but it took the latter some considerable time to regain her composure.

The dream, although not frightening, had borne an underlying menace, and Anna knew the perpetrator.

"O-Odin," she stammered. "It was Odin."

CHAPTER SIX

Once she had her emotions under control, Anna described the dream to her unsettled parent, concluding with, "Thing is, I don't think it's a dream in the normal sense. There is a familiarity about the scenario which has me questioning whether this is a memory, not a figment of my imagination. I know that sounds far-fetched, but..." she shrugged, and opened her palms — the gesture requiring no words.

Given that 'far-fetched' was par for the course in their lives, Sela accepted her daughter's theory without so much a raised brow, musing, "Ok, assuming you are correct, why? What is his motive?"

Anna pondered that, recalling Odin's sly tone. "I think he's trying to drive a wedge between you and Dad, and me, testing my loyalty. Especially, bearing in mind, he accuses Dad of killing the man Odin alleges was my father, in that existence. Unlimited power has always been his greatest desire, and he thinks everyone else wants the same; that the lure is impossible to ignore."

"Does he not remember what happened in the cave?" That Odin could possibly forget, floored Sela.

"If you had his ego, would you admit to being bested by a child?" Anna countered.

"Oh dear..." Sela and her daughter shared a wry grin.

The dreams continued for the next few days; each one more detailed than the last.

Mindful this was a deliberate ruse to bait her, Anna also wanted to uncover the All Father's end game.

Coupled with her classes, the hours wasted hunting for Odin, while trying not to let the torment he enjoyed doling out each night affect her, left Anna on the brink of exhaustion... compounded by Sela's mother-hen act in a bid to protect her daughter from the boogeyman.

Her head throbbing from lack of sleep and her temper frazzled, Anna sat alone in the student union nursing a cup of coffee. She had sent Sela to scour the campus for any trace of the damned Asgardian, and seized the moment to reach out to Jörmungandr.

While her brother could not offer any hint as to Odin's whereabouts, his calming influence assuaged some of Anna's disquiet.

"It is not me you ought to be asking." He chuckled softly at Anna's scowl. "Be careful, if the wind changes, you'll stay like that."

"Hardy har har." She fought the smile twitching at her lips, but the dimples in her cheeks betrayed her amusement.

"That's better, now get on with it, you know I am right."

Taking a sip of the heady brew, Anna dipped her head in tacit acknowledgement. There was only one person who would give her a straight answer.

The caffeine zipped along her synapses, reducing her headache to a dull thud. Closing her eyes, Anna concentrated on contacting her aunt.

Freya's response was shrill, "For the love of... how am I supposed to get anything done if the pair of you are inside my head. Are you *trying* to make it explode?"

"Stop being so dramatic, Freya." Sela sighed as her mind merged with the duo.

"Ya both know this is hard on me now my powers are so limited," Freya huffed. "Couldn't you just send me money for a plane—"

"Please, Aunt Freya," Anna interrupted a note of desperation in her tone. "This is important."

"Okay, sweets, what's got your knickers in a knot?"

Ignoring her aunt's weird, and presumably English, colloquialism, Anna said. "Tell me about Skadi."

Silence filled the connection.

Although Anna sensed Freya was still there, she could not help but stutter, "A-aunt Freya?"

"Why do you want to know about her? That giantess has been dead for more centuries than I care to recall."

"Because I need to know the truth about what happened to her," Anna explained.

"And what my bloody husband had to do with it," Sela interjected.

"Can the two of you hold your damn horses?" Freya berated. "And perhaps get yourselves somewhere more private than the middle of a university campus. I need half an hour." Abruptly, the connection was suspended.

Mother and daughter met by Anna's VW, the former bewailing the tight confines of the Bug.

"Why you could not let your father buy you a proper car is beyond me," Sela grumbled.

"Leave Bug alone, she suits me perfectly. Do you think I can afford a gas guzzler on a student's budget?" Anna retorted.

The pair bickered cheerfully while Anna drove to the university's cross-country course where it was quiet at this time of day.

"Ok, we're surrounded by nothing but trees and grass. Come on, Freya, spill." Anna sent the thought.

Both women got the impression, Freya was moving quickly, but couldn't figure out how, why, or by what means until they heard a whinny.

"Blizzard," the pair spoke in unison and grinned.

"Jack might know all about who I am... was... but he doesn't need it shoved in his face," Freya replied to their unasked question. "Okay, you want to know about Skadi?"

"*Yes*," Sela and Anna chorused.

"Ok, I'll need to go back a bit further, otherwise it won't make any sense." Corralling contrary thoughts, Freya began the tangled tale, making sure she was not *too* specific with regard to those involved.

"For once, I think Odin was being partially truthful, although I suspect he bypassed his involvement. He was correct in that Skadi wanted to avenge her father's death... for which she blamed the entire pantheon, not erroneously I might add, but it wasn't *quite* as simple as an innocent being killed.

"It would take me far too long to give you chapter and verse, and there have been several different versions of the Skadi myth in the sagas but, as I was privy to most of it, my version is the one you should trust, and stop rolling your eyes," she chided.

To Freya's amusement, she perceived Sela and Anna assuming angelic expressions. "Honestly, you two."

"But you luuurve us," Sela crooned.

"Hush and listen, I haven't got all day. So, going back to the beginning. A trio of gods, out in the wilderness... don't ask me why, I have no clue... stopped for a meal, but the earth oven they built did not seem to be cooking the meat. It transpired Thiazi, Skadi's father, in the form of an eagle, had perched in a tree above them and was preventing the oven from working. No idea why, maybe he was having a bad day." Freya gave the telepathic equivalent of a shrug.

"Anyway, they struck a deal; he would light the earth oven, if they agreed to share their food. Problem was, he took the lion's share, and you can imagine how well *that* went down. Honestly, spoiled children, the lot of them." Blithely ignoring the fact, she was still considered a deity, despite bequeathing her powers to Sela.

"Anyhow, instead of discussing it like rational beings, the gods lost their tempers."

"*Quelle surprise*," Anna's sarcasm made Sela choke on a snort.

"Don't interrupt," Freya warned. "One of them jabbed at Thiazi with his staff, Thiazi flew away carrying the god with him, who, after being slammed into boulders and trees and goodness knows what else, begged the eagle to set him down. Which triggered another bargain.

"For reasons no one could ever puzzle out, Thiazi wanted Idunn, guardian of apples and bestower of eternal youth, for himself, which meant agree or be pulverized. Not quite sure why the idiot god didn't just let go, or wait until the eagle grew weary and had to land... of course, that doesn't make a good story, does it?"

Neither of her listeners answered, presuming it was a rhetorical question.

"So, Idunn was duly lured from Asgard with the promise of better apples, Thiazi kidnapped her and whisked her off to Jötunheimr. Everybody's happy, yes?"

"Nope," Anna chimed in.

"Without their apple supplier, the gods began to age... and quickly. The deity responsible for Idunn's disappearance was threatened with a gruesome and protracted death if he didn't rescue her with immediate effect. He did, but Thiazi chased after him only to be caught and killed.

"Skadi, reasonably enough, was pissed off by this and swore to take revenge..." from this point, Freya's narrative aligned, more or less, with Anna's dream, studiously avoiding any reference to her own part in the debacle and, hoping neither woman pressed her for the finer details, wound up her tale.

Dead silence.

Freya could not even discern the sound of breathing, but she *was* aware of a confusion of thoughts and emotions.

Sela did not voice her intuition regarding Loki's involvement, but Freya had slipped up. Mention of a hungry god being thwarted along with a staff... too large a clue to be ignored.

"Dad was in it up to his neck, wasn't he?" Anna echoed Sela's suspicions.

"No more than any of the others," Freya prevaricated.

Anna recalled that long-ago conversation with her aunt, about them knowing each other in a previous existence... 'Even Jacob can't curb his curiosity over how quickly you took to hunting and the outdoor life'.

She knew from her research that Skadi was described as a beautiful strong-willed, frost giantess who — according to the sagas — became associated with winter, snow, hunting, skiing, and mountains.

Her fractured memories were akin to looking at a jigsaw puzzle which was missing those last few vital pieces to complete the picture.

"I know he, all of the gods, behaved badly — it's their stock in trade, but I need to know why I'm dreaming about this Skadi, and why I am seeing things through her eyes. I'm not an outsider watching the story unfold. I'm it. *I'm* the story, but it's not finished, like the last chapter got torn out or something." The girl's frustration zinged between them.

"No, love, it's j—" Sela started to reject Anna's assertion, when Freya spoke over her.

"That is the only rational explanation, although be warned, Odin is manipulating your dreams to his advantage. He has taken pains to gloss over his responsibility in instigating the chain of events."

Freya deemed it unnecessary to allude to the rumor that, eventually, Odin took the goddess of winter for his wife. She did *not* need Anna throwing up while their minds were connected.

"I think Dad and I should have a quiet chat." Anna's long-suffering sigh whooshed down the delicate link, almost severing it.

CHAPTER
SEVEN

"Would you be so kind as to get your head out of that mead and talk to me, Dad," Anna's *request* was less a plea from a dutiful daughter and more a command from an all-powerful being.

Primed by Sela, while Anna was occupied with Freya, Loki did not pretend to misunderstand the summons. "Give me five."

Placated, for the moment, Anna made small talk with her mom, waiting for her father to return to the telepathic party line.

What happened next nearly made her jump out of her skin and, already on high alert, prepared to lash the intruder with a volley of lightning as a thunderous pounding threatened to shatter the Bug's driver's side window.

Assured by his wife that she and their daughter did not have company, Loki chose to manifest at the cross-country course, instead of playing Freya's mind games.

Wearing a berry and honey-stained apron, resembling some crazed killer bee, the god of pranks was clutching a full tankard. His smug grin, indicated his pride in materializing without spilling a drop of the frothy liquid, currently threatening to slop over the battered rim of his pewter flagon.

Until he saw the faces of the duo in the car.

Unimpressed was an understatement.

"Really?" Sela sent him an incredulous look. "Couldn't leave that at home?"

"Hey, I was enjoying a quiet drink with Jacob on the deck. Not abandoning good mead." Loki twinkled at his two favorite women, still trying to dazzle them.

At their pointed lack of response, he shrugged and squeezed his imposing frame into Bug's backseat, nearly crushing his daughter in the process, not to mention dousing the two in the front seats in the strange blueberry and honey concoction as he did.

"It wouldn't go to wa... what am I saying?" Sela palmed her forehead. "Can you be serious, *ástin mín*? This is our daughter, not some demi-god after your stock of home brew."

"Okay, okay, you have my full attention," he rumbled and, nursing the remnants of his drink, made himself comfortable.

"Is this related to your dreams?" Loki ran an astute gaze over Anna's reflection in the rearview mirror, noting the weary cast to her features and lack of sparkle in her eyes.

"Mom told you?"

"There is nothing we do not share, sweetheart, especially when it comes to you." He smiled gently.

"You didn't..."

"*Check*? No. Geez, what do you take me for? I have no intention of invading your privacy unless I have no choice."

"Sorry, Dad, it's just..." Anna twisted her fingers

together and for a moment, looked like the ten-year-old child who curled up on her father's massive knee when she was feeling overwhelmed. It took everything Loki had not to repeat the gesture.

"Right, I want chapter and verse, from your dreams to what Freya told you and anything else you think might be connected, however insignificant. Some details, I already know, but I want to hear it from your perspective."

It took some time but, eventually, Loki was in possession of the pertinent facts, from the theft of the necklace, to Freya's revelations of less than half an hour ago.

Loki pinched the bridge of his nose, wishing — not for the first time — his mistakes would not keep popping up to bite him on the butt.

"Let me get this straight. You believe you are the reincarnation of Skadi, and that Odin is using your past life to drive a wedge between you and us..." he flicked his hand towards Sela, "for his own nefarious purposes, which *must* relate to a power grab?"

"In a very large nutshell, yes. Dad, what happened with Thiazi and Idunn?" Anna shuffled in her seat to look her father dead in the eye.

"Please, Dad. Even Freya was trying to protect you... and probably herself," she added dryly, "but if I am to defeat Odin, I need to know everything. Did you kill Skadi's father?"

Loki met Anna's troubled gaze.

He swallowed his fury that Odin's insidious insinuations, deliberately timed to shake Anna's faith in her father, had precipitated this moment. Loki was no fool; he couldn't avoid it, but had hoped to postpone it... a little longer. That his actions a millennia ago might cause a rift between them, tore at his heart.

Playing for time, he guzzled the last drops of mead, and wiped his mouth with the back of his hand.

Memories reared up in Loki's mind, and he relented. Anna deserved the whole truth.

"No, his death was not my fault, but I was not an innocent bystander either." Blowing a resigned sigh, and in typical Loki fashion, he filled in the gaps left by Freya.

"I was the one who struck out at Thiazi when he was gobbling the food. Just because he made the oven work did not give him the right to eat the lot. Talk about greedy."

Sela leaned back in her seat and arched a brow at her god-husband who considered a whole reindeer to be little more than an entree.

He caught her expression and, even if he had not, the disbelief was palpable.

"Hey, I always share." he jutted his chin in defense.

"Anyway, as I was saying before I was so rudely interrupted," he continued loftily, "I only intended to knock Thiazi away from the oven, but my staff kinda lodged into his body. The damn fool took umbrage and flew off, with me attached."

He shook his head in recollection.

"I hung on for dear life, took my poor feet weeks to recover from being dragged through the treetops. In the end I had to exhort him to set me down, I thought my legs were about to be torn off..."

"Why didn't you just let go?" Anna interjected. "You're immortal, the fall could not kill you."

"And lose my staff?" Loki's response was sharp. "Not bloody likely."

Anna's eye roll mirrored her mother's.

"He agreed on the proviso, I persuaded Idunn to meet him. Hey." He held up his palms at the matching black looks. "No way did I imagine he would kidnap her. I'm not that stupid. I was as shocked as everyone else when they vanished. Neither did I foresee the adverse consequences of her absence.

"Long story short," he refrained from mentioning the vitriol heaped on his head by an infuriated Norse pantheon, surmising... correctly... he would receive no sympathy from the two listening, "I rescued her, Thiazi followed me, and was killed by the gods."

"And Freya's part in this?" Anna pinned him with a steely gaze.

Loki hesitated, uncharacteristically unwilling to lower Anna's opinion of her aunt.

"Dad..."

Reluctantly, he admitted, "She leant me a cloak which allowed me to shapeshift."

"Into?" Sela asked.

"A falcon. They are among the swiftest of birds," he clarified imperiously.

"How did you get Idunn home?" Anna quizzed.

"Turned her into a nut," Loki said proudly. "Master-stroke that was."

There was a brief silence as Anna and Sela absorbed Loki's disclosure.

"Let me get this straight," Anna parroted her father's earlier remark. "If you hadn't tried to hit Thiazi, none of this would have happened?"

"If *he* hadn't been such a glutton, none of this would have happened," Loki countered mildly. "He started it."

Anna frowned, a caustic retort on the tip of her tongue. She pressed her lips together so as not to blurt it out, an odd sensation rippling through her. The peculiar intuition you are not alone, that someone is eavesdropping, but in her head, not holding a glass to the other side of the car window.

"Dad," she whispered, feeling her cheeks leach of all color.

In a flash, she found herself outside the vehicle, flanked by her parents, their arms around her.

Their minds melded and focused on the intruder. The *presence* seemed to swell, to rush at their barrier like a blast of arctic wind, but was no match for the trio and, although it felt like hours, seconds later, abandoned the attempt.

"Odin..." Loki hissed. "A wise man would concede defeat and retire quietly. You do not know what you have awoken."

The reply — a raucous cackle echoing in their ears.

Anna was trembling with rage, not fear. "How dare he? I should have left him to rot in Jör's cave."

"Don't beat yourself up. You were protecting the Nine Realms the best way you knew how," Sela comforted. "What I want to know is how he emerged? Who released him?"

"I can't be sure, but that annoying laugh didn't quite sound like Odin."

An ugly thought struck Anna. The how, she had yet to figure out, the why... not so much. "Pinkeye my ass, " she sniped. "I know where the old bastard is hiding."

Grabbing her parents' hands, the trio vanished in a flurry of leaves, to reappear outside the RA's room.

Hammering on the wood paneling, she bellowed, "Renner McDaniels, open this door now before I blow it off its hinges."

. . .

The commotion had every door within earshot yanked open. The various occupants were stunned to see the usually introverted and somewhat eccentric student from the third floor apparently breaking into Renner's flat, while her parents tried to restrain her.

The collective judgment was that the RA had managed to get another Freshman in some sort of trouble and was now trying to duck out on her.

Anna heard two blondes from the adjacent room speculating as to the extent of the misfortune.

"I'm guessing herpes," the taller one posited.

"You're so dumb. Her parents are here. It's gotta be a bun in the oven."

They both fell silent when Anna spun to face them wild-eyed, her fiery hair corkscrewing around her head like Medusa's snakes. Without uttering a word, the shorter roommate got the hint they should leave — immediately, suggesting, "Come on, Gina, let's go to the union and get some coffee."

Her roommate whined in protest, "You never want to have any fun, Shannon. Besides, I want to hear—"

Before Gina could finish her thought, Shannon hooked her by the arm and dragged her down the hallway, leaving the crazy redhead to her banging.

Sela pulled her daughter away long enough for Loki to use sleight of hand to pick the door's feeble lock.

Anna broke free of her mother's grasp, and charged through the door, only to pull up short, her senses protesting.

"Od... Renner, show yourself. I know you're here, I can smell your rancid hide."

"Anna," Sela chided, shutting the door behind them, "You need to control yourself."

64

"Yes, my daughter," Loki concurred. "Odin could be lurking in a corner, waiting to strike."

"Screw it," Anna retorted angrily. "If you want to end this, Greybeard, face me now," she addressed the fetid air.

No one answered.

Which did *not* mean they were alone. The longer they stood, the stronger the scent of rotting flesh became, coiling into their nostrils with each breath.

Tracking its source, Anna assumed she would come across a discarded meal. As the three drew closer, they discovered the sallow husk of the body which once housed Renner McDaniels and, as of late, Odin.

The flesh of Renner's face was stretched tightly over his skull as though mummified in a hurry by careless priests.

In place of his right eye, a bloodied hole above a shattered nose. His dulled and milky left eye seemed to glare at the trio in gruesome accusation.

His mouth, a tortured slash, marking the body's last breath.

Loki knelt next to the corpse, trying, as delicately as possible given his fingers were huge, to examine the body for traces of further damage. Regrettably, a mere touch transformed the empty shell into a heap of ash-gray powder.

The women skewered him with matching... *did you have to do that?* ...looks.

Brushing his hands on his jeans as he stood, Loki shrugged. "Looks like we are too late."

Sela scoffed, "You think?"

Ignoring her parents' customary banter, Anna spread her hands over the ash-like remains, swirling them into oblivion.

"Enough, you two, we have things to do."

EIGHT

As quickly as they had decamped from Anna's car, the three returned.

"Errr... why are we here?" Loki's head was spinning, not only from the mead. "Should we not be searching for that pestilence?"

"And leave Bug to be stripped for parts?" Anna huffed, patting the VW's hood.

"Now hop in, or go wait for me at my quad but, please, do not freak out my roommates. They might be annoying, but I don't want to be responsible for giving them heart attacks."

"As if," Loki's use of his daughter's default teenage response, pulled grins from the two women. "I'm not getting back in that tin can, I'll end up looking like a pretzel. Sel?"

He crooked his arm, and jogged his elbow invitingly. "You coming with me, or...?"

Sela dithered, unwilling to let Anna out of her sight, acutely conscious her firebrand daughter might go off half-cocked, but loath to voice her trepidation.

Her mother's unease made Anna raise her palms. "I promise to go directly to jail, I will not pass go, and I will not collect two hundred dollars." She chuckled, quoting from a board game they had played at Sela's insistence because she wanted them to share in activities enjoyed by 'normal' families.

She flapped her hands at her parents. "Go, I'll be there in about fifteen minutes, oh, and please don't destroy the campus in the interim," she added by way of a caution, and not wholly in jest.

Shortly thereafter, ensconced in the communal area of the quad, sipping coffee, and munching on chocolate chip cookies, the three tossed out ideas... from the sublime to the ridiculous, it must be admitted... to trap Odin and relocate him to the foulest, darkest, inescapable pit of hell.

"I wonder who his accomplice could be?" Anna mused, as she dunked a cookie in her coffee. "The one who released him?"

"Can only be a deity or a valkyrie," Loki replied. "No one else has the ability or the power."

Sela spouted proudly, "Given our baby girl here decimated them at Pine Ridge when she was eight, we can discard most of the valkyrie army. You should have seen her, Loki—"

Anna was quick to interject before her mother's train of thought derailed the entire discussion, "Mom, not the time for a trip down memory lane."

"Ok, that narrows the field, quite a bit." Loki chuckled. "Who do we have left?"

The three ran through the list of likely suspects, but agreed that releasing the All Father was not in the interests of any of them.

His apparent demise had come as a relief both to the terrorized pantheon, and the rulers of the Nine Realms.

To investigate Odin's doom suggested they preferred the lash of his tyranny to the unexpected amnesty his death had wrought. Being able to breathe without fear of losing one's life, far outweighed any lingering guilt at their unquestioning acceptance of his loss.

"That leaves the handful of surviving valkyries," Loki concluded.

Anna sent out a question to Freya who, presuming she was no longer needed had disengaged herself, and clicked Blizzard into a fast gallop across the ranch.

Grudgingly, she slowed the horse to a steady trot, and dragged her mind back to the *conversation*.

"Do you think I have nothing better to do than hold your hands while you figure out what ought to be blindingly obvious?" she muttered balefully. "Honestly, it's like teaching your grandma to suck eggs."

Despite the gravity of the situation, Anna spluttered with laughter. "Aunt Freya, say what now?"

"It's an English saying, meaning you already know, you just haven't the wit to see it. Come on, people, get with the program. Who possesses the gift to baffle, bewilder, and beguile. The only one able to block another's magic, or so she believes." Freya's tone of thought carried a hint of impatience.

Although she had faced a swarm of the winged witches, Sela could not name a single one, never mind their respective talents. "I have no clue," she said blankly.

"Good grief, woman." Freya palmed her forehead, literally and in her mind.

"Didn't you think learning who they are and what they

can do might come in handy given you're supposed to be protecting the peace?"

Before Sela could justify her omission, Anna piped up. "Myst. It has to be Myst. She's the only one better at obfuscation than Dad."

She winked at her father who feigned affront.

"Correctamundo, sweets. Right, now that's cleared up, you must excuse me, I—"

"Hang on, my darling auntie, ignoring your appalling imitation of the Fonz... where on earth did you? Never mind... might you be sooooo kind as to offer any hints as to how we can find Myst and her sleazy boss?" Anna interrupted.

"Hmmm, I imagine it will be rather like catching a shadow but, beware... shadows only emerge when there is light. In the darkness they have nowhere to hide," Freya offered cryptically.

With that she was gone, leaving a faint trace of some exotic fragrance and a vexed trio in her wake.

"Awesome," Sela expostulated. "Find a shadow? Thanks for nothing."

Silence descended, each concentrating on unraveling Freya's riddle.

Anna was moved to murmur that she was surprised the room hadn't burst into flames given the brain strain, only to be swatted by her mother.

"If you can't say anything constructive, zip it." Sela frowned at her unrepentant daughter.

"Sitting here is getting us nowhere. Okay, let's assume, I unsettled Odin when I gave him an ear-bashing about my necklace, or maybe he decided Renner's body was not worthy to house so noble a deity," Anna posited facetiously. "He will be on the hunt for a more suitable host, presumably one able to mingle with the student body unnoticed, or so obvious we would discount the likelihood."

"Can't argue with your logic," Loki said, unfolding his massive frame from the couch. "I need to stretch my legs anyway."

He reached out to pull up his wife and daughter. "Operation Valhalla's Doom begins."

"Wow, Dad, corny or what?" Anna teased.

Loki grinned down at her. "Can you think of a better name?"

An inexplicable warmth seemed to infuse the room, almost as though hope was revived, although a more practical mind might attribute it to the sun blazing through the window.

Anna and Sela exchanged a glance.

"Nope," they chorused cheerfully.

No one took any notice of Myst as she drifted across the bustling campus, hunting for satisfactory prey. She had discounted the other women in the quad because they were too close to Anna who would identify even the subtlest shift in their respective psyches, immediately.

It needed to be someone the brat trusted, but not a special friend or confidante.

Aware Renner's body had been discovered, Myst knew she needed to be careful. To underestimate Anna or her family would lead to unfathomable repercussions, which would, no doubt, incur her master's wrath. That she did *not* need.

Hours of fruitless prowling, her quest seemingly destined to fail, Myst was about to give up when a conversation, wafting out of one of the offices on a quiet corridor, caught her ear.

"Tomorrow, at 11 suit? Cheers, Anna. I know Professor Simpson is keen to discuss your proposal..." a long pause, "...sure thing, I'll see you then..." another, shorter, pause then, "...'kay, g'night."

Blending in with the decor, Myst crossed the threshold to observe the speaker. Had she been talking to her Anna or some random student who bore the same name.

Gliding closer, she peered at a curiously bound bundle of thin paper, the likes of which she had never seen before, which lay open on the table. It was covered with neat jottings, each against a number. Myst had an inkling, these numbers somehow related to the hours of the day, but that was sheer guesswork.

Alongside the 11:00, the woman wrote, *Anna Helsdatter - assignment proposal.*

Myst watched her use the writing implement, to shade out two lines, blocking off the section between the 11:00 and the 12:00, then wrote *Lunch* next to the 12:00.

With less than a whisper of air, and smiling slightly, Myst exited the office checking the door as she left, spying a name plaque, Ms. Shelly Connelly, and underneath, Teaching Assistant.

She had found her prey.

Hurrying to the outskirts of the campus, Myst settled under the sprawling branches of a tree, sent a silent message, and waited.

A faint shimmer and Odin was walking towards her — his physique peculiar, his attire rumpled and ill-fitting but intact. She could almost see the god's massive body rebelling against his current victim's less bulky frame — a poor unsuspecting janitor who was in the wrong place at the wrong time.

"Success?" he asked brusquely, without greeting her.

Masking her sadness at his indifference, Myst gave her report. "If you make your way to this woman's office during the period she has assigned as lunch, I think the professor will be there. I have work to do before then."

Getting to her feet, Myst stared at Odin, the fine line between love and hate never more apparent. *Maybe...* her heart held out hope even as her head taunted her naiveté.

Before Odin could question her intent, she was gone.

He glowered at the spot where the loyal valkyrie had stood. "Her usefulness is waning," he griped to himself, then looked up at the stars winking into existence as the purple dusk darkened to inky night.

Odin knew some civilizations believed the twinkling pinpricks of light were their ancestors keeping watch over them in tranquil radiance.

The celestial panorama above him, pulsed with a vastly different energy. Two stars, slightly brighter than their neighbours, seemed to exude unadulterated hatred.

"Bah," the grizzled god spewed, shaking off the crack-brained notion. "There's nothing but emptiness and gas out there."

His thoughts turned from the fanciful to the prosaic. "Tread carefully, Anna Helsdatter..." his smile was fiendish, "...the final encounter looms."

CHAPTER
NINE

With no clue who Odin had chosen to inhabit, the search party drew a disheartening blank.

As the sun dipped towards the horizon, hunger drove Anna back to her quad.

"You joining me?" she threw over her shoulder, knowing, at this juncture, her parents would not let their daughter out of their sight.

"Depends on the offer," this from Loki, the thought of food making his stomach rumble.

"Dunno, we could grab a pizza or burgers?" Anna suggested half-heartedly. "I'm too tired to cook."

"How about Irish stew?" Sela's offer was met by matching broad grins and expectant faces.

"Yay, does that mean a trip to Dublin? I haven't had Uncle Sean's stew in ages." Anna cheered, welcoming the idea of a brief respite from the turmoil plaguing them in Vermillion.

Her mother's expression conveyed a different story.

Blushing, Anna realized the error of her supposition, lamenting, "Oh, you meant, *you're* going to cook?"

"Yes, that is if you have the makings?" Sela replied, arching a quizzical brow.

Anna shrugged. "Not a clue."

"Fine, you leave me no choice. Let's hope your room-mates aren't home, or at least, not in the kitchen."

As luck would have it, the quad was empty, and Sela did not have to worry about her ingredients popping into existence rather than being extracted from the fridge.

Soon, the aroma of the rich stew permeated the room, giving Anna a sharp stab of homesickness.

For a split second, she questioned why she had left the ranch and everything she held dear.

It was all well and good, wanting a normal life, but she missed her family. *Not* that she was about to apprise them of this. She was not prepared to put up with her father's gleeful, "I told you so."

The evening passed without incident. Sela, noting the dark circles under her daughter's eyes, steered the conversation away from Odin, Myst, and Renner. That mess could wait until the next day.

The dream came again, but this time there was another layer. Skadi's aura, or whatever was communicating with and through Anna was stronger, more vital.

Memories, if indeed, they were memories, were coalescing but, although the jigsaw puzzle looked less fragmented, the picture remained indistinguishable.

"What?" she demanded irritably. "Are you me, am I you, or is this something else entirely? You do not smell like

Odin, and your aura is clean and white, not sullied. So, who are you?"

The voice... not even a voice, more a sensation, insubstantial as a draft... filtered into her slumber.

"We are two in one and one in two. I have spent an eternity adrift, awaiting my rebirth. I feared fate was mistaken, that the one destined to be Odin's Bane was naught but a myth.

"Then I felt you stir, the faintest glimmer of your essence, drawing our souls together, entwining our heartbeats."

Anna blinked, her gaze falling on the stark wintry landscape. By rights, it ought to feel forbidding, inhospitable, yet the emotion bubbling within her soul was quite the opposite.

In the distance, snow topped crags towered. Closer, dark green forests were shrouded in snowy mantles, concealing creatures of the ice. In front of her, leafless trees huddled in random clusters, the rime on their clawing branches — which stretched to the dazzling cerulean sky — sparkled like crystals in the sunlight.

Anna exhaled slowly. Her breath, a vaporous cloud in the frosty air as she whispered, "Skadi?"

The affirmation came into her mind like a feather on an eddy of wind.

Anna did not mention her nighttime encounter the next morning. She could not explain what stayed her tongue, but this fusion seemed too ephemeral and, in all honesty, she worried her mind was fabricating the union to fit Freya's revelations.

Discretion advised she keep it to herself... for a little longer.

Breakfast eaten and the quad tidied, after a fashion, Anna and her parents ventured onto campus, which at this early hour, resembled a ghost town.

Bleary-eyed students, fighting sleep and looking as though they had forgotten how to get dressed, blundered their way to class. Most grumbling about the lunatics who thought scheduling lectures at this hour was a good idea, and their own stupidity for thinking law/engineering/accounting... was a great career.

Behind the relaxed demeanor of the trio, every sense was working overtime, seeking even the slightest whiff of Odin or his traitorous valkyrie.

"I can't do this all day you know," Anna said, as they sat on a bench sipping strong coffee. "I have a meeting this morning and a lecture this afternoon."

"What time?" Loki, who had never really mastered the intricacies of clocks and watches, especially the digital devices everyone assured him were the 'thing', glanced at the sun to gauge its position.

Anna stifled a grin at her father's archaic time telling, then pulled a truly gruesome grimace.

"Eleven. I can't be late. It's with Simpson about my paper. I need his self-important stamp of approval. Then I've a lecture with him after lunch. I missed one last week, and can't afford to miss another. He'd use it as a way to lower my average."

"Would you like me to have a word in the right ear, poppet?" Sela asked, her face the picture of innocence.

Anna knew that meant bending some poor schmuck's mind to her mother's will, and shook her head.

"It's okay, Mom, I want to do this without magic, as far as possible. He might be a jerk who thinks he knows more about history than me, but he's also my Academic Advisor. I should, at least, try not to piss him off any more than I already have."

Swallowing an irreverent urge to giggle at her daughter's disgruntled features, Sela said mildly, "Do try to play nice, dear. Humans have an aversion to being made fools of. Makes them twitch."

"Yeah well, shouldn't behave like fools then," Anna grumped.

"If you're sure I can't help..." Sela let that dangle.

Anna shook her head. "I'm sure. Thanks for the offer." She hoisted her backpack over her shoulder and kissed both her parents. "I'm gonna head over to Shelly's office. Meet back at the quad for lunch?"

"Sounds like a plan. Stay vigilant, sweetheart," Loki cautioned.

"Bet on it, Dad."

With a grin and wave, Anna strolled off.

Sela, watchful eyes on Anna, shuffled along the bench to where her husband was sitting.

"He's going to be lurking where we least expect him, *ástin mín*. Can we observe without her knowing?"

"I can." Loki patted his wife's hand and without so much as by your leave, transformed into a bird, zipping over the crowds of students as he followed his daughter.

Sela cast a wary eye around the precinct, relieved to see no one seemed to have noticed a hulking great man vanishing into thin air.

"One day, Loki," she said drily.

Gathering the rest of their belongings, Sela wove her way through the swelling ranks of students, giving several a silent ticking off for barging into her while preoccupied with their mobile phones.

"Zombies," she tutted, smiling sweetly when they stared at her in confusion. "Another coffee methinks."

Shelly Connelly unlocked her office and, after hanging her handbag and jacket on the hook behind the door, deposited her armful of files on the desk, careful not to tip the coffee balanced on the top.

Her morning vanished in a flurry of phone calls, interspersed with diverting the odd catastrophe, and two student consultations which left her wanting to bang her head on the desk... hard.

Do I really need this job? Her daily refrain.

Regrettably, the answer was yes. Swallowing her irritation, Shelly did what she did best, and smoothed the waters.

Anna Helsdatter arrived, punctual as ever, followed shortly thereafter by Professor Simpson.

Conscious of the underlying tension, Shelly ensured tempers did not fray and, within twenty minutes, both student and Academic Advisor were on the same page... so to speak. To the extent that, their discussion became quite animated and remained, for once, amicable.

Masking her relief, and with a skill born of practice,

Shelly brought the meeting to a close, scheduling a follow-up two weeks hence.

"Goodness how the time is flying, blink and this semester will be over." She grinned at Anna who responded in kind as she picked up her backpack and waved a goodbye.

"I'll see you in class," Professor Simpson, perched on the desk, intoned.

"I'll be there," Anna's reply wafted back along the corridor.

From the farthest corner, Myst observed the teaching assistant.

Her relationship with Anna was relaxed and open without being familiar or obsequious, and it was clear Anna trusted the teaching assistant.

Perfect.

"I'll be back in a minute," Simpson said and hurried out.

As he left, the temperature in the room dropped, and Shelly could not prevent a shiver nor quash the strangest impression she was not alone. Warily, she spun around in her chair, chiding herself for letting her imagination run away with her.

Her back to the desk, Shelly's nape prickled, and ice slid down her spine. It was ***not*** her imagination.

Something was hovering, a beautiful illusion, reminiscent of a winged Victory.

Shelly blinked in disbelief.

This could not be happening.

The specter lunged.

Startled, the young woman gulped and opened her mouth... but her scream went unheard.

Myst shimmied to get comfortable in this interesting body, absorbing Shelly's sharp intelligence and dry wit.

Shame I cannot inhabit the female for longer, it would be fun.

She summoned her master.

CHAPTER
TEN

Anna fidgeted, restlessly. She loved history, but good lord, it was as though old Simpson was going out of his way to bore his class to tears. His usual passionate delivery was lacking, and his voice had assumed a kind of soporific drone.

Hypnosis...

Anna jolted upright in her seat and studied the professor with narrowed eyes, letting her mind reach out to touch his... ever-so gently, a butterfly's wing would have more impact.

She did not register anything suspicious, but was on her guard now.

Did Odin have the audacity to merge with one of the academic staff?

She tilted her head in contemplation.

Of course, he did. He would use anyone and anything to achieve his goal.

Common sense told her that Walter Simpson was too obvious a victim.

Odin might be many things, but a witless fool he was

not. If he was trying to trick her, using Simpson as his bait would be more likely to backfire than succeed.

Then again, he was interred for a decade, and prior to that had lost his reason.

Apparently engrossed in the professor's monologue, Anna ran a checklist in her head. None of her current lecturers or tutors stood out as suitable fodder for the god's subterfuge.

She extended the list, pondering the department's entire, and numerous, personnel.

Begrudgingly, she conceded that selecting Renner was a stroke of genius because, aside from the fact he was a sleaze, he moved in every circle, could go anywhere without anyone questioning him, and was connected to everyone in the faculty one way or another.

Someone with similar freedoms and affiliations would be the rational choice.

"Don't get cocky," she rebuked her nemesis inwardly — just in case he was within hearing distance. "That was not a compliment."

Anna tried to concentrate for the remainder of the class, glad when the tedious hour was up.

"That was the worst lecture he's ever given," one of her classmates grumbled as they traipsed out. "I totally zoned out."

There was a ripple of agreement amongst the group, puzzled at their professor's lackluster delivery.

"Maybe he's got a hangover," another student suggested. "Can you imagine Stuffy Simpson drunk?"

A bout of raucous laughter followed.

"Might be better if he was," a third interjected.

The group walked away, their mockery floating back to Anna, who leaned against the wall.

"Anything useful?" she cooed as a tiny bird fluttered through the door just before it swung closed. "It's okay, coast's clear."

Infinitessimally, the air seemed to loose clarity, then Loki stood in front of her. "Just being a good father." He grinned.

"Riiiight..." Anna smirked and pursed her lips. "Did you pick up anything odd?"

"Nothing, except your professor should bottle that lecture and sell it to insomniacs. How do you put up with it?"

"He's normally annoyingly animated.

"I wondered whether Odin was using his body to try to hypnotize us, although I can't understand why he'd bother, there's easier ways to trap the gullible, but I couldn't discern his presence at all."

"Neither could I. At least we can discount him, so not a total waste of time."

Anna didn't reply, not entirely convinced all was as it seemed with regard to the professor.

Odin stalked back to the office where Myst was ensconced.

"What on Midgard possessed you to choose this fool?"

He flicked a disdainful hand at the body he now inhabited. Professor Simpson's ego was more inflated than that of the luckless Renner... although, at least, he had good reason, which was more than could be said for the former Resident Assistant.

"He is the first person Anna would suspect, and therefore becomes the least likely," Myst appeased.

Odin frowned, but Myst gave him no chance to question her.

"Miss Smarty-Pants comes into contact with the professor frequently, therefore, for you to commandeer his persona is predictable. She will assume you would not be so blatant, meaning my choice is perfect."

Odin ruminated over this peculiar logic, a sly smile forming. "You have done well, little one. Now we need to bait the trap. Does this professor have a residence? Somewhere we can go, away from this..." his lip curled, "...cesspit."

Myst preened under his praise.

"I have discovered his abode is just off-campus, away from prying eyes. I have scouted its location and am happy to take you there."

"Can we not simply..."

For once, Myst was one step ahead of him. "Of course, but is it not sensible to maintain the ruse? By treading the paths of this curious establishment, we adhere to the expected behavior of these two people."

Conceding the sense in Myst's argument, Odin dipped his head. With Shelly's routine ingrained in the valkyrie's head, Myst — while unsure of their purpose — collected a handful of files, a bag, and a jacket.

Anyone passing the pair, winding their way along the spider web of paths leading to the gates and beyond, could not have conceived the chaos they were plotting.

As they skirted the library, Myst spotted the shelves of

books visible through the windows. She marveled at the number.

"My lord," she exclaimed. "Is it not incredible that, despite the lackadaisical lives of these Midgardians, they possess the talent for literary creativity?"

"Bah," Odin groused contemptuously. "Nothing but irrelevant drivel. The vast majority is stolen from ancient history. While in my time—"

A blur of movement to his left prompted Odin to turn in time to see Myst sprint off at breakneck speed towards the library's front door.

"Mys...err..." for a split second, Odin had forgotten the TA's name, resulting in confused stares from a student or two.

"Ms. Connelly, what in the blazes are you doing?"

The question hit Myst's ears in time for her to point to a second-floor window before darting into the building.

She could not believe her luck. *Have the Fates reversed their judgment of Odin?*

Looking up, Odin thought he saw Anna Helsdatter, carrying a veritable tower of books which obscured her face, quickly realizing it was a case of mistaken identity.

"No, you impetuous child. Wait."

As Myst's prey approached the top of the staircase, Odin spotted his acolyte already halfway up. The valkyrie's intent — painfully obvious.

Deliberately, Myst collided with the student sending the young woman down the stairs, her arms flailing help-lessly. Books sailed in all directions, hitting other students crowded around tables below.

With a wild shriek, and in what to those who witnessed it seemed like slow motion, the student bounced on the unforgiving concrete, slamming into a step near the bottom. She lay, sprawled silent and still; her body buckled, her neck at a grotesque angle, blood oozing from her head.

Odin did not need to be in the building to know the young woman's neck was broken.

His angry gaze jerked to the top of the stairs where he saw Myst standing, mouth agape, the ramifications of her error dawning.

Concentrating, Odin heard, through Myst's ears, horrified screams echoing from within the library, as the onlookers registered what had occurred.

He saw people congregating at the top of the stairs, shouting, "Shelly Connelly, what the hell have you done?"

He watched as Myst, unable to meld into the shadows, fled from the upper floor before any could stop her.

You will be punished for your disobedience, you imbecile, the All Father warned the valkyrie, not caring whether she heard him.

Outside, Odin caught up with Myst as she burst out of the door on the far side of the building.

The wail of sirens pierced the air, galvanizing the pair.

They vanished.

CHAPTER
ELEVEN

S ave the light cascading from his *host's* cold box,
darkness surrounded Odin. He had lost track of the
number of trips he had made here since Myst and he
had sought refuge in this dwelling.

He cursed his companion for acting of her own accord.
Her misguided attempt to take matters into her own hands,
had compelled them to use magic to effect a rapid escape
before the police arrived. A course of action which could
reveal their location.

"Damn you, Myst. How could you be so brazen? I told
you to stay away from the monster," he growled into the
empty room.

Multiplying the misery, from the moment Odin
invaded the body of Professor Simpson — over and above
the wealth of knowledge about Midgard he was now privy
to — he had suffered from an insatiable appetite. In his
previous life, food and drink provided not only suste-
nance, but also had been a source of fellowship and
pleasure.

The hunger he was experiencing, currently, was like a

relentless itch. No matter how much he ingested from the box, the more he desired.

Odin could not be sure whether the cause originated from the years he had been locked away, and forced to do without...

...or...

"Does this human actually possess an appetite which rivals that half-wit Loki?"

Reaching into the chilly storage cube, he snared a rosy apple from a bowl, at the same moment as the clock in the hall chimed two.

He froze.

If there was anything in this or any of the Realms, Odin feared, it was time itself and, listening to the old clock tick away the seconds of life from the mortal he was inhabiting, he swore he felt himself withering.

Closing the door, Odin took a seat at the large, flat-surfaced piece of furniture in the middle of the professor's domestic quarters, and bit into the apple, savoring its flavor. Not as sweet as Idunn's fruit, and definitely lacking any of the age arresting benefits, it was still tasty.

The irony that he was munching on the very fruit which had played a pivotal role in an unfortunate sequence of events, the detrimental impact of which was only now surfacing, was not lost on him.

Looking down at the apple, Odin faced an indisputable truth. He needed to return to Valhalla, posthaste, no matter the cost. There he could devour Idunn's life-giving bounty to his heart's content and transform Simpson's body into something more suited to the All Father.

For some reason, recalling his life in Asgard, while trapped in Midgard, made Odin feel old.

Memories flooded his mind.

Of how he and his brothers, Vili and Ve, had slain the jötnar, Ymir, to rid Yggdrasil of any beings who might be more powerful than he. An act which had, inadvertently, led to the creation of this confounded realm.

Of banishing Loki's daughter Hel to Helheim because he sensed she too possessed the power to overthrow him, even though she had never made a move against him.

Tired and frustrated at his introspection, Odin bellowed, shaking the foundations of the house, "Enough of this self-pity, old man.

"And damn you Loki for breeding offspring destined to challenge me," Odin grumbled, sinking his teeth into the crisp fruit. "I should have killed you the first time we met."

The click of a switch was loud in the quiet, and the fluo-rescent glare of the kitchen light made him blink. His thoughts scattering like chaff in the wind, Odin looked up to see the form Myst was borrowing, standing in the doorway.

Rubbing the sleep from her eyes, she yawned. "Is there a problem, my lord? I heard you shouting something."

"No, little one, just reminiscing."

"It is late, my lord. Please return to the bedchamber and sleep. You must be fully recovered in strength to defeat Anna."

Rising from his chair, Odin agreed, "You have become smarter in my absence."

Soundlessly, he opened the drawer in the kitchen island, spying the dull glint of a large chef's knife.

"What say we celebrate your maturity and share this delicious fruit?"

Myst could not believe Shelly's ears. In her entire exis-tence, she had never received a gift from Odin. He always deemed others more deserving.

"I-if it pleases you, my lord. I would never refuse such a generous offer."

"Then come stand beside me, Myst."

Without a second's thought, his faithful minion did as he bade, and waited, hand outstretched, to receive the morsel.

"I pledge, All Father, to never take action against your enemies without your blessings."

Halfway through slicing the apple, Odin paused to smile at Myst. "Fear not, little one, never again shall you be forced to decide anything.

Pulling the knife from the apple core, he plunged it into Myst's breast. With the proficiency of a warrior who had spent eternity wielding every conceivable battle weapon, he eviscerated the human housing Myst's essence, until she could no longer stand.

Myst lay in a mutilated heap. Slowly, her tear-stained gaze traveled the length of the body harboring the malignant god, coming to rest on the tip of his knife, drenched in her blood.

Her soft voice fading and laced with sobs, she beseeched, "W-why must it end this way, my lord? Have I not served you to the best of my abilities? Have I not devoted my life to you?"

"You may have gained insight, Myst, but you failed to grasp the wisdom which should have accompanied it."

Odin's tone was ruthless, "I cannot risk you making another disastrous mistake. Take heart, wench, you will continue to sustain me in death."

"How can I be of any use, if I am dead?"

"Observe," was the last word Myst would ever hear.

Odin leveled his hands over her paralyzed body.

Closing his eyes, Odin stripped Myst's inherent power,

bestowed on her at birth by the Norns, along with her life force.

The intensity of anguish at her master's betrayal wrenched a garbled scream from the throat of his once obedient servant. Her body convulsed violently into a snarled arch before crumpling back onto the floor.

For the first time, his hunger was satiated.

Nonetheless, he finished cutting Myst's piece of apple. Balancing it on the crimson smeared blade, he brought it to his lips and, mockingly, acknowledged his faithful disciple's *sacrifice*.

"To my... *our*... victory."

Leaving Shelly's body where it lay, Odin walked through the pool of blood oozing across the floor, to the back door, dark red footprints tracking his steps.

The cool night air was refreshing, and he inhaled deeply.

Silence surrounded him as he felt the remnants of Myst's magic meld with his, bringing a sudden influx of uncontrollable energy which welled upwards through his body, spiralling out along his arms to his hands, and exploding from the tips of his fingers.

Its force reduced a swath of the woodland behind the house to smoldering stumps and ash.

This was a power he had never experienced.

At that instant, Odin recognized its source.

Throughout the decade clasped against his immortal enemy, a portion of her power had leached into his stone prison. Evidently, something even Anna had not noticed.

"I guess the little bitch is so full of herself, she had no idea she was nurturing me. What is it these human authors love to write... you create your own enemy."

He savored Skadi's age-old hatred of him as it brewed with the potency of Loki's offspring.

Facing the house, Odin reduced the structure to a blazing inferno.

The Fates' panicked screams filled his ears, as they felt not only the rebirth of the Asgardian's power, but also the overflow of his anger, and ruthless desire to reclaim his place within the Norse pantheon.

"That's right you traitorous hags, there will be hell to pay for your betrayal."

TWELVE

A nna lay in her bed caught between slumber and consciousness. She hated this space, it was where Odin tormented her; her brain unable to defend itself properly.

She was shuffling onto her side, praying sleep would drag itself over her when a command exploded in her ear.

"Skadi, wake up."

Failing to recognize the voice, Anna roared back, "Whoever you are, you have the wrong person. My name is Anna Helsdatter."

"In this life, maybe," the voice argued. "But I know my own daught—"

"Hold it right there, mister. My father, Loki Fárbautison, is asleep in the next room. All you have to do is shut up and listen to him snor—"

"How cruel," the speaker retorted angrily, "Why would the Fates be so merciless as to tie you to that oaf?"

"Look, if this is Odin, save your breath. There are no words in the tongues of Old Norse, Midgard or the Nine Realms which will trick me into severing ties with my family. I see right through you. I *am,* after all, the daughter of the prankster god."

"Skadi—"

"*Anna.*"

"Whatever."

Anna nearly laughed at the modern counterargument coming from whom she presumed to be supposedly long-dead ancient being.

"If this is not Odin, tell me your name. Otherwise, I'll let my parents track you down and mete out vengeance, the likes of which you could not comprehend."

There was a pause.

An image of a giant eagle popped into Anna's head. In its talons, the great bird clutched a staff, although Anna could not see it clearly, making it impossible to identify.

"My name is Thiazi, son of the jötunn Ölvaldi, and the father of Skadi... *you*. Do you not remember how they toyed with your heart after they murdered me."

"I know the story of Thiazi and Idunn. You weren't exactly guiltless."

"An argument for another time," the voice... Thiazi... dismissed. "More importantly, do you believe I speak the truth?"

"I'm not saying anything at the moment but, if you are indeed Thiazi, my dad and Aunt Freya already told me the whole sorry fiasco was instigated by you."

"Of course, the witch would cover for that degenerate mass of flesh," Thiazi countered.

"Listen, it's late and I have neither the stamina nor the desire to continue this ridiculous discussion. Tell me what you want and be gone."

Thiazi wanted to slap Skadi awake, but he had no idea to what extent *his* daughter existed and which part of this Midgardian belonged to the daughter of Loki.

"Odin is restored to his former strength. The Fates summoned me to warn you."

"Are they so useless, they are not aware my family knows Odin has escaped—"

"Loki's child, hush your prattling and allow me to speak to my daughter."

Fed up with this birdman, Anna was preparing to jettison him to the nethermost reaches of Niflheim, when she heard another voice cry out.

It was the female, Anna had discovered only recently. The one who prowled in the farthest recesses of her consciousness. The one who, suddenly, deemed it imperative she advertise her presence.

"I hear you, Father and, believe me, I have been trying to get this child to listen to me from the beginning of our shared time." The gentle voice had a testy edge to it.

"It is crucial you make her understand we must act with celerity. Odin has already left a trail of death in his wake. There is no telling how soon, he will track you down."

"Hey, I'm right here, " Anna butted in crossly.

As though Anna had not spoken, Skadi hissed, "Let him. I have waited too long to avenge your death, and to exact restitution for being added to his vile harem. Odin's concept of compassion. Ass," she finished with a scoff.

A dull throb niggling behind her eyes, Anna broke in sharply, "Enough."

Father and daughter fell silent.

"I hate to interrupt this heartfelt reunion between the two of you, but you need to stand in line and wait your turn to seek retribution. Mine comes first."

Thiazi and Skadi sighed in unison.

"What makes you think your cause is any more just than ours?" Thiazi chided Anna.

"I witnessed Odin executing my Dad..."

"And I didn't?" Skadi sniped.

Anna scowled, "...and repeatedly threaten to murder my family. I cannot let that go unpunished."

Once more it was Skadi who stated the obvious, "You had the chance to rid the Realms of Odin, but you just had to keep that shiny stone, you damn magpie."

"Now hold on one moment—"

"No. You hold on," Skadi retaliated sternly. "Time is of the essence, so, do me a favor, *child*, and let the adults finish their conversation."

Anna's research on the female warrior had revealed that she, like Anna's mother, was not to be trifled with. Instead of attempting to win control of the situation through a war of words, Anna tried another tactic.

"Look, this argument is getting us nowhere. You bestowed your power on me before birth, ipso facto, *I* am the one in charge of where and when we go anywhere."

That shut Skadi up.

"Good, now I have your undivided attention as well as, hopefully, your cooperation, let us devise a workable plan, and please send your father away for the time being, at least. I think he and my dad would be more hindrance than help."

Skadi's reply quivered with sadness, "B-but I have had no chance to talk to him since that terrible day."

Her words struck a chord with Anna, who thought she had lost her own father the day after she was born. Despite, subsequently, regaining an ephemeral contact through the void, the lack of Loki's physical presence during her childhood had left an emptiness in her soul.

Settling back against her pillows, Anna stared up at the ceiling.

After a protracted pause, she said, "Knock yourself out."

"Why would I injure myself?" Skadi retorted, confused.

Anna chuckled. "It's a figure of... never mind. It means please enjoy some time with your father."

A warmth coiled around Anna akin to a grateful hug.

"Thank you, Anna," Skadi murmured.

"Just make sure the two of you keep it brief. I need my beauty sleep."

With that, Anna eased toward the back of her consciousness, and raised a barrier in her brain to allow daughter and father to become reacquainted unhindered. It was like listening to the distant drone of a radio and... oddly soporific.

"Anna?" The voice, scarcely a sigh in Anna's brain, was enough to rouse her from a deep sleep.

"What is it, Skadi?" Anna replied in her mind.

"Thank you, again, for granting me time with my father. Even though he was hardheaded, I loved him."

"No need to explain." Anna smiled. "I reckon our dads are both cut from the same troublemaking cloth. Now you've had your family reunion, any suggestions as to our next move?" she added drowsily.

Skadi chuckled. Even for a female, the intensity was such, it left Anna's ears ringing and dispelled the last vestiges of slumber.

"Ugh, how about toning that down a little," she begged.

"My apologies," Skadi lamented. "I have found little at which to laugh for an eon."

"Excuse me for asking, but how is that in any sense, humorous?"

"Are you not supposed to be the most powerful being in existence?"

"So, I hear, but Odin is still Odin and, from what we just heard, his strength is increasing."

"And your blood runs with the tenacity of a formidable queen and the magic of two savage deities... even if one of the latter is a total jerk."

"Hey, watch it. That jerk is still my dad."

"Fine, fine. We have more important things to do than quibble over who's the bigger jerk. Do you think we could leave this room without anyone noticing?"

"Given it's the middle of the night, I doubt there's many people around and, I don't know whether you've noticed, but I can do one better. What do you have in mind?"

"You get us to that curious little horseless carriage you call Bug, and we will go from there."

"I'd really like to know before I step into any traps."

"Stop with the chit chatting, the clock's a ticking," Skadi scolded her new partner in crime lightly.

"Chit chatting?" Anna queried. "Was that even a thing back then?"

"I have endured your thoughts for the last nineteen years, and am not about to let any of them go to waste." The words were accompanied by the sensation of an unrepentant grin.

"You've *what?*"

THIRTEEN

Anna materialized behind the wheel of her Volkswagen, lecturing Skadi about the right to privacy, pretty sure it was falling on deaf ears... even if they were her own ears.

Before that made her head spin, she turned the key, the engine purring to life.

Skadi braved, "Are you done?"

"For now," Anna relented begrudgingly, switching on the headlights.

"Then can we get going?"

"Um, when you let me know where?"

"Oh..." Skadi chirped. "I don't know about you, but I'm hungry."

"Hang on, you dragged me out of my warm bed in the middle of night to *eat*, and since when do you get to decide my mealtimes?"

"Since I think better on a full stomach. How about we go to the cute little inn where all the students gather."

"You're gonna need to narrow the field, we're talking thousands of students here, there are several popular spots.

An image formed in Anna's head.

"The Flat Earth Pancake Shop? Wait, *you* are the reason for my recent pancake craving and the unaccountably altered astrophysical view of the world, which insists on popping into my head," Anna quizzed.

"I have no idea what astercycle means," Skadi butchered the scientific term, "as for their pancakes, more please, and their coffee... best discovery you Midgardians ever made."

Anna chuckled. "Thank the Fates I am not pregnant."

Despite Skadi's ribald laugh being in Anna's head, it was so loud, she was sure anyone nearby must have heard.

"Girl, you have to be sleeping with someone to worry about that."

"Hey, there's such a thing as Immaculate Conception," Anna protested.

"Riiiight because that happens with frequency," Skadi countered derisively.

"Whatever," she echoed Thiazi's earlier remark, with a wry quirk of her lips. "Okay, now hush and let me drive. Last thing I need tonight is to bang up Bug because you are distracting me."

Reversing out of her parking spot, Anna nosed the car through the university with the utmost care and kept her speed just under the limit, across Vermillion to the all-night eatery.

While the streets were relatively quiet, the restaurant was buzzing.

Most of the customers had either reeled in after the bars closed, or were long-distance truckers taking a well-earned break.

Needing to verify Odin was not among them, Anna *scanned* their minds, relieved to find none posed any threat, while checking out the pictures adorning the walls.

Some were movie stills of UFO's, others were flying saucers stacked with pancakes, zooming through space, and the rest were drawings of a squashed Earth and Universe.

Anna heard a shout from behind the counter, "Hi, Skadi. Grab the table in back and Molly will be with you in a couple."

"Sure thing," Anna heard herself reply adding, "How's the battle going, Xavier?"

"Same as usual, doll. The non-believers refuse to listen to the truth."

Baffled, Anna let Skadi lead the way to an empty booth in the farthest corner from the door. Sinking into it, she demanded, "Care to explain?"

"When you were blowing off—"

"Blowing off?"

"If you want an explanation, do not question my choice of words. You were *neglecting*," Skadi amended facetiously, "your Earth Science midterm, so, I... ummm... kind of brought you here to study. One thing led to another and we became somewhat of a regular."

"*That* explains those odd occasions when I woke up with sticky fingers, thinking I'd drunk maple syrup in my sleep. How about using cutlery next time you get a midnight craving." A brief pause. "Better yet, stop coming here altogether."

"B-but we have enough points for a free meal. Check

your bag."

Rifling through the backpack, she had the foresight to grab before she left the quad, Anna found a crumpled frequent customer card, ten ink stamps filling the bottom line.

She stared at it. *Now*, her mysterious weight gain made sense.

Inwardly flipping Skadi the bird, Anna tossed the coupon on the table, then dug out a lever-arch file and a couple of markers.

"Play nice," Skadi cooed, echoing Sela's remark of the previous day.

Ignoring that, Anna opened the file and pushed a few papers around, for all the world as though settling in for a few hours' quiet study.

Molly, the aforementioned waitress, approached the table. "Evening, hon. Same as usual?"

"*Usual?*" Anna enquired of Skadi.

"*Hush.*"

Before Anna could request a soda, Skadi replied, "Yes, please."

"Okay, two stacks of chocolate chip pancakes, bacon... crispy, and an extra-large cappuccino."

Molly jotted down the order. "I wish I could eat like that and not gain weight."

Anna chuckled internally, "Don't we all."

Shortly thereafter, Molly returned balancing a tray laden with food, the quantity of which would have made Loki raise his brows and, once served, meant no one would bother her for an hour or so.

Skadi remained in the recesses of Anna's mind leaving the college student 'alone' with her ridiculous mountain of pancakes and crispy bacon.

As Anna took her first mouthful, the contentment drifting through her as she savored the syrupy treat elicited an involuntary smile.

"Happy now?"

"Bliss."

While Anna devoured the fluffy deliciousness, the pair reviewed their situation.

Still processing the knowledge, she was also Skadi, Anna hurled a barrage of questions at the goddess who had occupied her mind since her conception.

Conversely, so many seemingly unrelated, insignificant, and previously inexplicable things suddenly made sense. *Aunt Freya was right... as ever.*

"Why did you wait until now to introduce yourself," Anna queried.

"You had no need of me. It was pleasant to loiter out of reach on the fringes of your subconscious, learning about this strange realm. Once Odin was eliminated, and other than ensuring you were not in immediate danger, I had no responsibilities. Of course, had you left..." she could not help but tease.

"Okay, okay, don't you start," Anna grumbled. "I do not know what prompted me to pick up the stone, it was instinctual. I might argue it was not a mistake, but who knows?" She shrugged. "I cannot undo it."

She could almost hear Skadi ruminating over that.

"There is always a reason for your actions, of that, I am convinced." Skadi's tone was meditative. "If you were induced to pick it up, it was preordained, meaning, this is also preordained, which is a comforting notion."

"I think you and I have differing ideas about what comforting means," Anna countered grimly.

Skadi smiled gently. "It is comforting because you,

personally, have not instigated this confrontation. It was decreed before time itself began. Had you left the stone on the floor of the cave, it would still have found its way into your possession. The Fates do not always control destiny. If they did, I would not be here."

"I wish I could ascertain his whereabouts. I know he is lurking, waiting to pounce, but I cannot perceive him."

The internal conversation went back and forth for some considerable time. Anna topped up her coffee, once... twice and, fighting exhaustion, was on the verge of giving up for the evening when Fortune — feeling magnanimous — smiled down on her.

A group of students, looking as though they had just crawled out of bed — and had forgotten that pjs are generally not considered acceptable attire when out in public — came into the restaurant.

On closer inspection, they were scruffy by design not default, and their conversation was anything but slovenly.

Seeking a table big enough for all of them, they came closer to Anna's booth, nodding their heads when they saw her apparently buried in study.

"Never stops, does it?" One of them, spotting her USD hoodie, winked in long-suffering complicity.

Anna grimaced her agreement. "Nope..."

As they dragged out seats, and sat down in cheerful rowdiness, Anna fought against the frown forming, aggrieved her peaceful corner was no more. She began to tidy her papers.

"...couldn't believe it."

"...did you see the cops and EMS... all that blood."

The group shuddered collectively.

Anna pricked up her ears and her hands, hovering over the file, stilled.

"...must have been some kind of breakdown. No one seems to know what triggered it."

"...she always seems so, ya know, normal."

"...academics, weird bunch."

Heads bobbed all around.

Anna shoved everything in her backpack and slid out of the booth. Passing the table, she said casually, "Sorry to interrupt guys, but what's happened?"

As one they gawked at her. *How could she **not** know?*

"You been living under a rock?" One of the girls, who was trying too hard to be a goth, sneered.

Anna sent her a withering glance. "For the last coupla days, yes... got a paper due."

More nods, this time in understanding.

"Gotcha," another sympathized.

"Don't be a bitch, Pip," said the guy who had winked, then looked at Anna.

"Fuck off, Brad," the girl, Pip, shot back.

"Shelly Connelly knocked a student down the stairs, killed her." Brad continued as though Pip had not spoken.

"I'm sorry, what? Shelly Connelly? Teacher's assistant, Shelly Connelly?" Anna could not believe what she was hearing.

"You know another Shelly Connelly?" Pip drawled belligerently.

Anna ignored her, never taking her eyes off Brad.

"The very same. Some of us were there." He flicked his hand towards one or two in the group. "It was bizarre. She ran up the stairs like a lunatic, and barged into Leslie, the student," he clarified.

"Books went one way, Leslie went the other. Next thing, she's dead on the stairs, and Shelly's done a runner. Not surprised, mind, she'll be facing murder charges. No way she can say it was accidental."

"Drugs," a third guy — who Anna recalled was in a few of her classes, she thought he was called Aaron — chimed in. "Has to be."

"Or demon possession." Pip chuckled nastily. "She'll find a loophole."

"Always cup half full, aren't you?" Brad stared at her, his expression cynical.

Pip flushed and scowled at him. "Bite me." She slouched in her chair and folded her arms.

"God, I just saw Shelly earlier. I had a meeting with her and Simpson. She seemed fine. No way. You sure it was Shelly?"

"Hard of hearing as well as slow on the uptake?" Pip mocked under her breath.

"My hearing is perfect, thank you." Anna smiled sweetly, a dangerous sign.

Don't even think about it, Skadi cautioned.

Too late.

Without warning, one of the legs on Pip's chair snapped, tipping the sullen young woman onto the floor.

The two sitting either side, helped her up, as Anna coaxed the rest of the story from Brad. In fact, he did not know much more than he had already shared, but he was flattered by the attention of this flame-haired beauty, and wanted to eke it out as long as possible.

"Thank you, Brad. Poor Leslie, how awful, and what a shock for her family."

There wasn't really anything else to say. Anna had not known Leslie and, although sorry she was dead, any outward show of grief would come off as affected.

She noticed Molly approaching with a tray piled high. A

good time to leave.

"Enjoy your meal." She turned to walk away.

"You could be cousins?" Aaron mused.

"Beg pardon?" Anna stopped and spun slowly on her heel.

"You and that Leslie chick, you look alike."

"No, they don't."

"Yeah, they do, both red heads..."

"Oh, so that means they look alike. What about all the blondes? Do they all look alike? Honestly..."

A heated debate ensued.

Anna left them to it, waving a goodbye to Brad and, childishly, sticking her tongue out at Pip, unaware of Xavier's speculative gaze.

Unlocking Bug, she climbed in, and sat there, lost in thought.

"Penny for them," Skadi teased.

"I think we just got our wish."

As they drove back to the dorms, the blare of fire alarms shattered the quiet, and flashing red lights lit up the night.

Neither Anna nor Skadi took much notice.

It was late, or early, depending on which way you looked at it, and a carb crash was threatening.

Besides, in a college town, there always seemed to be something on fire. A trashcan carelessly set ablaze by a discarded cigarette, some drunken frat boys' bonfire getting out of hand or, and rarely, a house.

All of which were someone else's problem.

FOURTEEN

"Mom, Dad, wake up." Anna burst into the quad like a miniature tornado, rousing her parents who were fast asleep in the communal area, one on each of the two couches.

Sela shot upright, glittering swords appearing in her hands as she surged to her feet.

"What? Is he here...?"

"Mmmpnerpphhhh," Loki mumbled incomprehensibly and pulled the blanket over his head.

"Sorry, Mom, no he's not here, but I know where he is."

Sela kicked her husband's butt, and sank back onto the sofa, the swords vanishing.

"Loki, get up. A lot of use you are to our daughter. What if Odin *was* chasing her?"

His response, a garbled curse in old Norse, then Sela's admonishment registered and Loki lifted his head.

"Odin?"

He unfolded his impossibly large frame from the two-seater couch and glowered.

"Where?" His question was delivered in a voice so deep,

the word thrummed through the bodies of the two women in front of him.

"Not here. Sit down." Anna pushed her father lightly on the chest and he dropped back against the cushions. "Listen."

She told them all she had gleaned, adding, almost as an aside, that Skadi and she, "had... err... melded."

In any other family, this admission would result in a hasty trip to a psychiatric clinic, in fear their daughter was succumbing to some kind of multiple personality disorder. In *this* family, it did not even cause a raised eyebrow.

Before Loki could interrupt, Anna continued, "I think it was Myst not Shelly, at least Myst in Shelly's body, who shoved that poor girl down the stairs. Apparently, this Leslie resembled me and, from a distance, it's not inconceivable, Myst could have mistaken her for me. Extending that thought, I believe Odin has purloined Professor Simpson's body."

"But you said you couldn't sense him?" Sela frowned.

"I think that has something to do with him being close to me for a decade."

"Go on," Loki said, beginning to see where this was going.

"Okay, bear with me because I know it sounds fantastical. I've worn the stone imprisoning Odin since I picked it up from the floor of Jör's cavern. What if the reason I do not sense him is because somehow, I have imbued the stone with some of my energy, like wearing perfume, and the overriding aura is," she paused for dramatic effect, "mine?"

That her parents did not refute her declaration, confirmed Anna's suspicions.

"I knew something was off with Simpson yesterday, but I assumed he was maybe hungover or coming down with something. I only questioned it because he was fine when I met with Shelly and him an hour earlier. You didn't pick up any Odin-like vibes did you, Dad?" She glanced at Loki who shook his head.

"See, and we assumed Odin using Simpson was too obvious, but that's exactly *why* he chose him. Myst must have worked out, I would never suspect Shelly and she's Simpson's TA. It's too huge a coincidence to ignore. Now it seems Myst, as Shelly, tried to kill me this afternoon in the library."

"But you were here after class," Sela interjected, trying to quash the fear Anna's rather nonchalant statement stirred up.

"Right, but *Myst* didn't know that, and now another innocent victim has paid the price for Odin's obsession, although Renner was not exactly innocent."

Anna sat back on her heels and beamed at her parents. "It fits. It's the only logical conclusion, and remember what Aunt Freya said about catching shadows."

"Catching shadows, *pah*. Your Aunt Freya is too enigmatic by half," Loki griped. "She could simply tell us, but noooo, where's the fun in that?"

"Let it go." Sela elbowed her husband, who raked a hand through his unruly hair and huffed a sigh. "I know Freya's exasperating, but she was trying to help not hinder. If she had any conclusive evidence about Odin, she'd share it, you know she would. We gotta do this without her."

Anna listened to this exchange, as Freya's words ran through her head... *beware the shadows, in the darkness they have nowhere to hide.*

Then darkness was where they would meet, where this would end, and where *he* would spend eternity.

She smiled.

It was time the tables were turned.

For the next couple of days, the trio could find neither hide nor hair of Odin, Myst, Simpson, or Shelly.

Sela and Loki resumed their search of the university grounds and surrounding community, insisting Anna continue with her classes.

Of all people, it was Loki who reasoned, "Your education is more important than squandering your time with Odin. If your mom or I find him, we will expedite his demise."

"B-but Dad—" Anna strove to persuade them that a repeated semester was no big deal. Everybody did it.

Her parents were united in their refusal to be coerced.

"The future will be yours to guide, and the more knowledge you have, the better equipped you will be able to handle whatever is thrown your way." Was their emphatic answer before they left to begin their patrol.

It was futile to argue. Once her parents had made up their minds, no amount of argument — rational or otherwise — could sway them.

While apparently, albeit temporarily, safe from Odin, life at USD had yet to return to normal.

Word had circulated that Professor Simpson's house was torched, scant hours after Shelly pushed Leslie down the stairs.

If the rumors were to be believed, the explanation was simple.

Shelly Connelly must have caught her educational meal

ticket, namely Walter Simpson, shagging Leslie Havers... in his office, no doubt. A woman scorned and all that.

Between lectures, and hoping to avoid the headache-inducing babble of her gossipy classmates, Anna ducked into the Student Union to grab a coffee.

No reprieve could be found there.

She happened upon a heated conversation led by Scott, a part time EMT who was in her English class.

As he, unnecessarily, provided his expert opinion regarding the course of events, he let slip that fire investigators had discovered human bone fragments after the fire was extinguished.

"From what I heard, the intensity of the heat indicates it was set deliberately, but they have yet to establish the type of accelerant."

Another student pressed for more information about the bones. "Are they Simpson's? He's missed class the last couple of days, and nobody's heard from him."

Scott shrugged. "They're sending them to the state Forensic Lab in Pierre for DNA testing. Guess they won't know for sure for a couple of weeks."

"I saw Connelly's folks on TV last night," someone interjected. Anna saw it was Pip putting in her miserable two cents.

"They were begging the wacko to turn herself in before she hurt anyone else. They should just follow the inevitable trail of dead bodies." Her lip curled disparagingly. "I always thought she was too good to be true."

Anna was sorely tempted to break Pip's legs, instead of just her chair's, but Skadi intervened.

"She'll get her comeuppance, Anna," Skadi reassured placidly.

"It can't happen soon enough."

Instead of going straight back to the quad, Anna opted to head into town to buy groceries. Loki had devoured the contents of the refrigerator along with most of what was in the cupboard, and the magic required to restock was too much to conceal.

Taking Bug would be easier and, much as she found traipsing around the supermarket a chore, leaving campus would be a welcome change.

Skadi interrupted Anna's *relocation* to the VW. "Can we get an order of waffles, too? There's a neat little place downtown—"

"Geez, Skadi, have you ever thought of asking before you take me somewhere?"

"You mean like I just did?"

The two bantered back and forth like sisters as, unde-tected, Anna vanished from the empty hallway to emerge in the small car, not registering that, instead of sitting behind the wheel, she was in the passenger seat.

A gravelly voice broke into their internal conversation, "You know these little metal carriages are endlessly fascinating."

Anna jerked around to see 'Professor Simpson' in the driver's seat.

Instinctively, her hand reached for the door lever, to hear the locking mechanism engage.

"Tut, tut, child," Odin cautioned. "Stay put. Otherwise..."

"Otherwise, what?" Anna fumed.

"This," Odin glanced at a group of students waiting to

board a bus, picked the obvious athlete from the herd, and snapped his fingers.

The occupants of the bus and the students on the sidewalk, watched in horror as the jock dropped to the ground.

A girl screamed, "Stevie, hon? **Stevie**? Oh God, he's not breathing. Someone call 911."

Appalled at his callous disregard for the sanctity of life, Anna gawked at Odin. "What the hell? Why did you do that?" she demanded wrathfully.

"It is very simple, child. I am the All Father. Life or death is at my discretion and I do not have to justify my actions. Every last creature inhabiting the Nine Realms answers to me." He thumbed his chest. "If your treacherous parents failed to teach you that... what is Skadi's excuse?"

An almost imperceptible gasp escaped Skadi.

"Ahhh, greetings, jötunn. Yes, you duplicitous whore, I recognized your repulsive essence on this Midgardian long before my imprisonment, even if *she* remained ignorant. No matter. Clearly, the Fates have granted me the gift of killing two birds with one," he paused and sneered, "stone, so to speak.

"That said, I am not a complete ogre. As long as he gets help quickly, Stevie ought to recover but, if you prefer me *not* to reduce the rest of his coterie to ash, I suggest you sit there and shut up. We have things to take care of."

He touched the ignition, and Bug's engine fired into life.

"I do believe Freya would have been better served by this machine instead of those recalcitrant cats of hers."

"Hardly," Anna retorted. "She's more a classic muscle-car woman."

"I have no idea what that means." Odin scowled as he ground the transmission into reverse.

"Hey, watch it. Don't vent your spleen on my little car. I just replaced the clutch."

"Quit your yammering, I have observed enough inhabitants of this realm maneuvering these metal wagons to know what I am doing. Moreover, my host is well practiced at the art."

On any other day, Odin's peculiar blend of modern colloquialisms and ancient phraseology would be amusing.

Not today.

Bug lurched forward as Odin found first gear. He revved the motor, and the car peeled out of the parking lot in a plume of gray smoke.

CHAPTER

FIFTEEN

Weary from their abortive trudging, Sela and Loki pushed open the door of the quad, expecting to see their daughter curled up in front of the tv. Her classes finished hours ago and, although she had mentioned she might pop into town for groceries, she ought to be home by now.

There was no sign of Anna.

Ice trickled down Sela's spine and, exercising extreme caution, she reached out in her mind.

A flicker, nothing tangible, then, almost like a camera shutter being pressed too quickly, a flurry of images burst into her head.

"Odin," Sela hissed malevolently. "The bastard has Anna."

Loki did not question his wife's assertion. Her unease was enough warning something was amiss. "Where?"

"I cannot tell, but he is controlling her by threatening the lives of a handful of unwitting students. We can do naught but wait until she is able to send more details."

"If you think I'm going to sit here like some kind of

impotent deadbeat while that weasel tries to consume my daughter, you are addled." Loki paced the room. "Where would he take her? Back to the cave? Would he risk that?"

"It does not feel like Jör's lair, but it is somewhere dark."

Sela glanced out of the window. The afternoon was waning, but the sky was bright and the sun had not set.

"I cannot discern whether he is inside a building, or..." her brow furrowed, "...beyond Midgard."

Loki's expression lowered. "Beyond Midgard? Surely..."

"He is Odin." Sela's tone was fatalistic. "His lust for power has blurred the last vestiges of his wisdom. He wants what Anna stole and will use every means at his disposal to retrieve it."

She held her husband's infuriated gaze. "We cannot rush in half-cocked, *ástin mín*. That will place Anna in more danger. We need to trust her. She's no longer a child."

Sela exhaled a resigned sigh. "Let's face it, she was never really a child. Everything in her life has been leading to this confrontation. In our heart of hearts, we knew Odin was not vanquished that day in Jör's cave. His body died but he is a god, *the* god. It will take more than a broken neck to seal his doom.

"Perhaps if I feast on his still-beating heart." Loki gave a wolfish smile.

Despite the gravity of the situation, Sela chuckled. "Always the warrior. Come, we ought to eat. I do not want you fainting from hunger when we face this madman."

A quick wave of her hand, and a pile of food appeared on the kitchen bench, including something resembling a dinosaur's thigh.

"Moose!" Loki fell on the delicacy with unabashed glee.

The darkness was complete.

Not even a pinprick of light cleaved the pitch black.

Nowhere for shadows to hide.

The air felt heavy and tinged with an indefinable emotion, as though weighed down by the combined burdens of the Nine Realms.

"You asked for it," Skadi murmured into Anna's mind.

"Not helpful," Anna replied in the same vein.

"Welcome to your destiny," Odin intoned. "Enjoy the last moments of your pathetic life. I guarantee, they will be as painful as I can make them."

Amused, Anna dipped a curtsy, mocking, "Why thank you, Oh Great and Illustrious One. I have been looking forward to this for millennia."

"To think we were once handfasted," Skadi seethed under her breath. "I rue the day."

"You assume, I care a fig for your opinion," Odin addressed Skadi scathingly. "A goddess by decree not by birth, who skulked in Thrymheim among the parched rocks where she could hear the wolves howl." This last, delivered in a jeering whine.

"You do not possess the strength to aid this puny deity. Your winter arrows will do no more than tickle. Do you intend to *ski* me to death?"

Odin's sardonic laughter grated on Anna's ears and she felt Skadi's fury building.

"Patience, Skadi," Anna exhorted inwardly, refusing to be impressed that Odin knew of one of the modern skills associated with her other self. "He is goading us, do not bite."

"Behold..." Odin's voice vibrated like a struck gong, the sound bouncing off an unseen barrier to ripple back in soft peals.

Imperceptibly, as though a gossamer veil was being drawn aside, the unforgiving inkiness lightened to reveal... nothing.

Gray desolation, more empty void than anything substantial, shrouded in darkness.

Anna was not game to move, expecting the ground beneath her feet to fall away into a bottomless chasm.

"Your damnation awaits." A parody of a grin split the deranged deity's face in an ugly slash. "Do, please make yourself comfortable. You will be here a long time."

Channeling Sela, Anna spat, "Bring it on you urchin-snouted, hag-born, swag-bellied carbuncle."

"It will be my absolute pleasure." Odin gave a flourishing bow and took one step to the side.

Behind him, a slightly darker shade of murk than its surroundings, a huge boulder, skirted by a narrow strip of something flat.

Anna squinted.

Resembling an abandoned track, the strip had no vanishing point, there was no horizon.

Dread clawed at the periphery of her consciousness and, without moving her feet, angled her upper body to peer the other way. Freya's caveat echoed in her mind, *beware the shadows.*

She knew... *no*...she had heard of this place.

Sela had deemed it unwise to divulge the whole story of what she endured on the road outside Niflheim; the abridged version was horrific enough.

The nightmares she had suffered after the telling reared up in Anna's mind. This was purgatory or, at least, it had been.

She recalled her mother explaining it had been a hell of her own making, a waking terror symbolizing the futility of her existence. Sela's craving for power and her obsession for revenge had blighted her soul until it was as black as the maw.

The same maw in which she, Anna, now stood.

How was this possible?

Her brain whirled with the connotations of Odin's chicanery, but she kept her expression bland.

She had no intention of spending a single minute here, never mind eternity.

He was trying to trick her. He was always trying to trick her.

"Why here?" she asked, sounding no more than vaguely interested.

"A fitting end, do you not agree? I am closing the circle. A soul for a soul." Odin studied his prey meditatively, flexing his fingers and bunching his shoulders in readiness.

While the monumental ego of the once venerated god had long eclipsed reason, his thirst for victory remained undimmed. A lethal combination, for there was no counter-balance.

If this homicidal maniac was not stopped, permanently, the consequences would be cataclysmic. Not just for Midgard, but for every one of the Realms.

There would be no salvation.

Acutely aware it might well cost her, her life, Anna inhaled a steadying breath and embraced her destiny.

It was time.

"You with me?" She sent the fleeting question to Skadi, sensing the ancient goddess nod in response.

"We must prevail."

"Then we must fight as one."

Without waiting to see what Odin was playing at, Anna opened her palm to launch the first salvo.

The creeping darkness obliterated the flare of the explosion, but not before the fireball, landing mere inches from Odin, illuminated his form.

Contemptuous laughter boomed around them. "Need a little light, you miserable mongrel?" he barked.

"Perhaps this will help your execrable aim." The All Father summoned up his power, allowing it to it suffuse him until his whole body radiated with the brilliance of the sun.

His return volley, compelled Anna to execute a kind of wild shimmy to avoid being struck.

"That's it, girl... dance for me."

His taunt fueled Anna's ire, but she banked it down.

"I presumed your father and his slut of a concubine had trained you to be a more worthy opponent."

"I'm just warming up, old man," Anna snarled.

The battle to decide the fate of the Nine Realms began in earnest. Neither gave any quarter, each absorbing the other's magic with every attack.

The two deities were well-matched.

Anna heard Skadi screaming at her to conserve her strength. Odin's plan was one he had honed over the centuries. *Let your opponent defeat himself.*

Desperately, Skadi tried to reach Anna, but it was as though a gulf was widening between the two entities. Without warning, she found herself afloat in the endless depths of oblivion; ripped from Anna's consciousness.

Her devastated howl ought to have deafened anyone within hearing range, but there was no response.

Only stillness... and pain.

In despair, Skadi sent out a plea to the only one who could help.

If he was listening.

CHAPTER
SIXTEEN

Far above the Nine Realms, twin stars glittered in the cosmos. Observing without judgment.

Flung into the heavens in a belated act of reparation, they had hung for millennia amidst the constellations... silent sentinels.

Admired by stargazers throughout the centuries, associated with many myths, and referred to by many names... in Midgard they were known as Castor and Pollux.

No one knew their genesis. No one knew these were not simply stars.

An anguished petition crossed the great divide, stirring the guardian from his eternal repose.

The two stars blazed.

This was no ordinary invocation. To ignore it would precipitate the fracturing of the world... of all the worlds.

The time for watching was over.

"For shame, Odin. Did you not realize, your petty vengeance would come back to haunt you?"

In a quiet quad, Sela was stacking the dishwasher while her husband bagged up the trash.

He was about to take it out when his wife husked, "Loki,"

"I'll be two ticks," he said without turning.

"Loki."

Something in her tone made him pause. He glanced over his shoulder.

Sela's face was pinched, her pallor more akin to that of a cadaver than a healthy goddess.

"*Sela*."

He dropped the bag and shot across the room to steady her as she swayed on her feet.

"What is it?"

"Odin is killing our daughter, and Skadi's aura is detached from Anna's. **Worse**... the void. He has recreated the void." She could smell the sickly sweet odor of decay, and hear the clank of manacles. The ghastly nightmare prowled menacingly.

Oh hell no.

For the first time in a decade, Sela felt tears brimming. She blinked them back fiercely. Now was not the time to succumb to a bout of weeping.

Loki could not prevent the string of ancient Norse profanities — some, even Sela had not heard — along with a litany of tortures he would like to impose, which tumbled over his lips.

His quick apology and obvious remorse brought a

tremulous smile to his wife's lips and, effectively, quashed lurking sobs.

"I agree with your sentiment, and would delight in exacting several of your proposed penalties, but first we have to find them."

"How? If this is a horror of Odin's mind, where do we start?"

"Pray to the gods, I may hold the key. Take my hands..." Sela instructed, "...and trust me."

Their fingers entwined, Sela let her mind meld with Loki's.

She reached through his memories to the altercation with Thiazi... possibly the source of this whole catastrophic debacle. Then, came forward with head-spinning rapidity to her servitude on the rock.

She slowed the images. The answer had to be here, it *had* to be.

Then she saw it.

The faint glitter, as a small golden disc was flipped.

Skadi's unexpected absence left Anna bereft, as though half her soul had perished. Along with it, she felt a dip in her magic.

What part of 'we fight as one' did you not understand? she groused to the ether.

Figuratively straightening her spine, and pulling her power around her like a suit of armor, Anna threw all she had into her firestorm, but it was taking its toll, and she acknowledged Odin was gaining the upper hand.

Across the desolation, the deadly encounter continued unabated, its brutality seeping into the Nine Realms, whipping up ferocious storms which ravaged vast swathes of land.

A bolt from Odin pierced Anna's shoulder, spinning her around. Fortunately, the searing heat cauterized the wound before she lost too much blood.

Odin was toying with her. His strikes calculated to injure, debilitate, and weaken, not to kill. Not yet.

Anna was baffled by the ease with which the aged Asgardian countered her onslaught, especially given she was supposed to be the most powerful being in the universe... in every universe. Odin moved with the speed and grace of an Olympic athlete, despite being shelled within Walter Simpson's dissolute body.

The throbbing pain in her shoulder hampered her concentration and, for a split second, she took her eyes off her opponent.

Next thing, she was flat on her back, the wind knocked out of her, a spurt of gyrating dots marring her vision.

"Oh, what a surprise, Skadi has left you in the lurch. Betrayed by your cherished jötunn ghost. Seems avoiding a second death takes precedence over saving your measly hide. Spineless coward." Odin jeered over her prone figure. "Fret not, she will be joining you in eternal damnation soon enough. First, there is this paltry matter to wrap up."

Anna gulped in a lungful of air and, pleased to note all her limbs were, almost, intact, leaped to her feet.

Convinced victory was within his grasp, Odin unleashed his fury, pummeling Anna with a torrent of violent blows, so fast they were naught but a blur.

Abruptly, Anna's mind was inundated with scenes from their first battle. Assuming it was Odin trying to distract her, she was about to shove them aside — *what use was this memory?* — when she recognised the source.

It was Jörmungandr. *What was he doing?*

A light bulb flashed in her head.

She could not defeat the All Father because she was, essentially, fighting herself.

Well dammit.

To block the flying fists was futile, she needed a different tactic. Scouring her brain for something, *anything*, to thwart his barrage, Anna remembered a move her grandfather had taught her years before.

Lowering her arms, she left herself vulnerable to Odin's onslaught.

Anna's apparent capitulation confused Odin. *Was the the bane of his existence on the verge of surrender, ready to yield to her fate?*

A vicious snarl contorting his face, he drew back his elbow ready to strike. He could taste his triumph.

Seeing the arrogant glint in the All Father's eyes, Anna knew the slimy reprobate had taken the bait.

Before Odin could inflict his deathblow, Anna, with lightning speed and with all the strength she could muster, slammed her hands against his ears. The percussion ruptured his eardrums, the impact propelling him across the dirt.

Dizzy, his ears ringing, Odin heaved himself upright, glaring at his opponent, who was also bleeding profusely.

The struggle for supremacy was not over.

Before the dueling deities could resume hostilities, high above, a beam of vivid iridescence erupted. From a tiny point beyond their gaze, the single ray flared to pool around them.

Intimidated by the dazzling golden glow, the pitiless void retreated.

Blinded by the radiance, Anna squinted in an attempt to focus on the origin of the light. Ignoring the discomfort, she made out the lazily pirouetting shape of Sela's coin.

Which could only mean...

Through the incandescence, hazy shadows shimmered and took shape. There was something dearly familiar about the silhouettes, and a wave of relief surged through Anna when her mother and father materialized, using their bodies to shield her from Odin.

Another voice, melodious and feminine, yet uncompromising and indomitable, reverberated from every corner, "Now, Father, finish him."

Spontaneously, three pairs of eyes widened, prompting a wary Odin to glance over his shoulder. His startled gaze landed on Thiazi, standing begin him, staff at the ready.

What new madness is this? Who has conjured up the dead?

Pivoting on his heel, the All Father gaped in stupefaction at the giant, who looked very much alive and who, with a flick of his wrist, twisted the aged wood to reveal a point of polished steel.

An incantation to expel Thiazi, hovered on Odin's lips, but he never uttered it. In one fluid movement, the giant rammed the spike into Odin's open mouth, and out through his neck, shearing his spinal column.

Jerking the blade with vicious intent, Thiazi chuckled at the sound of Odin's vertebrae cracking, rendering Simpson's body useless, trapping Odin inside.

As Odin crumpled to the ground, he saw Skadi appear next to her father.

"Is everything ready for the new guest?" the giant asked, a smile warming his craggy, but oddly beautiful, features.

"Yes, father and, from what I gather, Hel is looking forward to welcoming her new resident. Seems she has some unresolved business with our friend here."

Disbelief swept across Odin's face as he registered the fact that, by some miracle, Hel had survived his murder attempt and was waiting at the end of the road.

Winking at Anna, Skadi shared the image of Odin's final destination.

It was the nebulous penitentiary, concealed in a schism between the Realms, into which Hel had conveyed Loki after his battle with Odin, the night Anna was born. The curiously ephemeral yet impregnable 'chamber', upgraded in readiness for the disposal of Odin's doomed body.

At its entrance, her half-sister, Hel.

Why she did not cross back into the Nine Realms was a mystery to Anna but, presumably, Hel had her reasons — no doubt the most important being charged with giving the perfidious Asgardian a taste of his own medicine.

Ann was surprised when Hel gave her a friendly wave.

"Please tell Father I'm fine," she requested. "Who knows, maybe one day, you and I might have a chat over coffee."

"*Coffee*?" Anna smirked.

Hel shrugged. "Blood, coffee... choose your poison. Not necessarily literally."

"I'll hold you to that, Hel," Anna vowed with a grin.

Anna ensured Odin was privy to the conversation regarding his impending sentence, taking special delight in dangling the possible reconciliation between half-siblings in front of his nose. Each facet demonstrating, unequivocally, that his vengeance had failed.

Odin's unmitigated horror when the dreadful truth dawned, engulfed her, eliciting a hysterical guffaw, and leading her parents to question whether the protracted strain had broken their daughter.

Sela and Loki gathered Anna close, their love beginning to heal the trauma.

Thiazi studied the All Father.

Placing his boot on the disgraced god's forehead, he wrested the spike free from Odin's skull.

The carcass containing Odin, the once all-powerful god, began to fade, and Thiazi cautioned, "Remember your manners and be sure to greet your new Mistress properly... *veslingr*."

The threat of Odin relegated beyond hope of return, a somewhat disparate family returned to the quad, a peculiar feeling of anti-climax setting in.

There was half-hearted mention of a celebratory meal, but Anna had class the next morning and Sela deemed it unwise to disturb her daughter's roommates at this ungodly hour.

Skadi trilled, "I know a good panca—"

"Not a chance," Anna vetoed with unexpected vehemence, much to her father's disappointment.

"Maybe another day, my daughter," Thiazi placated his equally dispirited offspring. "We need to return to Niflheim, or we will receive a terrible rebuke for missing dinner."

"Huh?" Sela asked dumbfounded before Skadi could get a word in edgewise. "What are you doing there?"

Thiazi rumbled humorously, "I seem to have inherited the place from Hel. No one else wanted it and, according to her, the underworld cannot run itself. Chaos was standard there but, left to its own devices, became chaosier? Is that a word?"

Skadi did not bother to answer that question... a more pressing one required clarification. "*Who* is expecting us for dinner?"

"Oh, did I neglect to mention your new stepmother? I must have forgotten in all the excitement."

Skadi huffed, "Ya think?"

Her indignation made Anna chuckle. The rekindling of the father-daughter bond between Skadi and Thiazi reminded her of when Loki and she first tried to negotiate the same relationship.

"Are you going to clue me in on who it is, or do I need to play twenty questions?" Skadi implored.

"Idunn agreed to be my wife. Over the years, we straightened out a few things and, to be fair, she was homeless. It took some adjusting, but we made it work, and Idunn was able to reestablish her orchard?"

"In *Niflheim*?" Loki was astounded. Aside from the fact, Idunn's fruit was partially responsible for creating this slippery slide, surely Niflheim was as infertile as the void they had just escaped. "How is that possible? Is it not far too cold?"

"Funny thing, when I was removing the moldering carcasses left by your daughter, I unearthed a thermostat. Who knew? Once Idunn had adjusted the temperature to suit a garden instead of a boneyard, her trees began to flourish. I dare say it is almost paradise there now, and could explain why Hel refuses to visit.

"Oh, and on the topic of cleaning up that dumping ground, Loki," Thiazi addressed his one-time nemesis, "I would appreciate you collecting your crap. Hel's altar to you is, well, pretty disturbing.

"Take it all, except this, of course." Thiazi twirled the staff, a sly smile twitching at his lips.

Loki blinked and blinked again.

"*Laevateinn*."

It was the very weapon, Loki had spent a lifetime crafting. He had poured so much blood, sweat, and tears hewing the intricate design into the wood — not to mention the concealed spike — the Norse had bestowed on it, its own legend.

Thiazi chuckled, "So, you do recognize this battered piece of oak. Found it being used as a towel rack."

"Hel would no—"

Thiazi tapped Loki on his chest with the knob, worn smooth over the centuries. "Rest assured, she would not, although I am unsure why it was under her throne. Maybe she used it to smack her unruly subjects on the head."

"Knowing Hel." Loki grinned broadly; with his child anything was possible.

As the adults made their farewells, Anna approached Skadi. "Will I ever see you again?"

"Do not worry." Skadi smiled. "I will hear you if you need me, and shall not be gone for long."

Cheered, Anna went to give her a hug, forgetting Skadi was in spectral form, the pair laughing when Anna tripped through her.

"I'll fix that before I return," Skadi promised.

"Make sure you do," Anna admonished. "I expect you back before next semester. I have a nature study course, and I'm gonna need your expertise."

"It's a deal... as long as pancakes are involved."

SEVENTEEN

Three Months Later

In the aftermath of the traumatic events, Anna became something of a recluse.

Time had not diminished the endless gossip about what happened to Shelly, Professor Simpson, and Renner McDaniels.

What was the old saying? *Tales grow taller with the telling.*

The stories surrounding their disappearance circulating around the campus ranged from the absurd to the preposterous. Including a love triangle, a menage gone wrong, academic jealousy, abuse, and everything in between.

Unable to enlighten anyone, Anna struggled to concentrate when it seemed to be all her classmates wanted to talk about. Even the library did not offer an escape, being the epicentre of the drama.

It was the juiciest scandal ever to hit USD, and the entire student body intended to eke out every last titillating detail... for as long as they could get away with it.

Neither did Anna have Skadi, who had been an integral part of her life, to talk to. Her parents, along with Freya and Jacob offered an ear and a shoulder when needed, but Skadi was a part of her, and she missed the connection.

The only place Anna found any refuge was... to her chagrin, and ignoring Skadi's gleeful mirth... the Pancake House. As the semester ticked towards the Christmas break, she was often leaning on the door waiting for Xavier to open up.

Gradually, the pair went from a cursory greeting to passing the time of day and, almost without realizing it, became comfortable chatting about all manner of things, surprising Anna who tended to have several firewalls around her privacy.

The year turned and, to Anna's well-concealed relief, Skadi kept her promise.

Just how the goddess had applied and been accepted to USD, Anna had no clue, presuming — correctly as it happened — the requisite paperwork had been produced by sleight of hand. That they were together again was enough.

While university rules required Anna to remain on campus until the end of her second year, the same did not apply to Skadi. Her *reported age*, elevated Skadi to the status of mature student, and she was granted permission to live off campus.

After spending a reasonable portion of Anna's first semester scouring Vermillion in search of Odin, Sela and

Loki had become conversant with the city. This made it easy for them to find Skadi a suitable apartment in a decent neighborhood, with a second bedroom in case Anna needed a bolt hole.

Bending the rules, as ever, Anna stayed at the apartment more than she did the quad and, despite *cozy* being the kindest description of the unit, the pair loved it. Having their own place far outweighed the lack of space.

Something Thiazi was thankful for, preferring the duo watch out for each other.

Anna's former roommates did not object to her absence. As much as they liked Anna's parents, her father's enormous appetite and her mother's over protectiveness could be awkward. That said, their brief visits — more for show as Anna was rarely there — were welcomed with open arms because they never arrived without masses of treats.

Skadi settled in quickly, immersing herself in all things university related, including, once the coach had witnessed her expertise in winter sports, being persuaded to join the Alpine Ski Program.

Slowly, Anna's natural vivacity resurfaced, her eyes began to sparkle again, and she looked less drawn.

Her friendship with Xavier flourished, their conversations verging on the personal. Anna was not naive, she had seen the interest flaring in Xavier's eyes, but she gave him no hint she wanted to be anything more than friends.

Skadi, who knew there was more going on, insisted Xavier was a top bloke and wouldn't try anything stupid.

"Come on, Anna, I've known him longer than you. He's never shown any interest in any of the other girls until he clapped eyes on you... even though it was me dragging you there. Not even when I went there as me did my astounding beauty have any effect. How rude." She feigned affront, then grinned. "Go on, hon, why not take a risk?"

"Give over, Skadi. He's not my type."

"You mean drop dead gorgeous isn't your type?"

"You noticed, huh?"

"I'd be blind not to. He has his own business, which is booming... so he's doing something right. Bit of a kook with the whole flat earth thing, but beggars can't be choosers." Skadi chuckled.

"Hang on though don't you... didn't you... I don't want to..." Anna faltered, unsure how Skadi felt about Xavier.

"You worried, I fancy him? Nah, I checked, no passion. He's cute, but I prefer blonds."

"You *checked*? No, don't tell me. Anyway, this discussion is irrelevant, I don't have time for romance."

"Boring," Skadi interrupted with an exaggerated eye roll.

And so, it went on. Skadi teased Anna. Anna ignored Skadi.

Until the night Anna's tongue ran away with itself.

It had been a long week; papers due, mid-term exams to be studied for and, by the Friday evening, Anna was overtired. Skadi invited her to a ski club mixer, but Anna declined, saying she was going to take a shower and have an early night.

One look at her friend's weary features and Skadi didn't push. "I won't be late," she said an hour later, as she dashed out, dolled up to the nines. Anna grinned at how easily Skadi had embraced twenty-first century fashions.

In the blissful quiet of the apartment, Anna indulged in her longed-for hot shower, changed into her pj's, and climbed into bed, wishing there was a way to tranquilize her brain without resorting to sleep aids.

Hyped up on study, not enough rest, and sugar, slumber remained elusive.

In the end, with an aggravated huff, she flung on jeans and a hoodie, hopped into Bug, and drove across town to the *Pancake House*. Carbs and coffee, that's what she needed, blithely ignoring the fact, caffeine was why she couldn't sleep in the first place.

"Coffee, triple strength, *stat,*" she called theatrically as she opened the door.

"What's up?" Xavier asked as he whipped up her usual.

"Can't sleep."

"Wanna talk about it?"

"You wouldn't understand." Anna was unaware of the wistful note in her voice.

Xavier studied her contemplatively.

He had waited for this moment since Anna's arrival at USD.

What began as an irritating task, after a not-so-subtle request from his mother to keep an eye on Anna from a discreet distance, had become a labor of love.

He had never felt this way before, and battled against the all-consuming emotion, declaring it to be nonsense, until Skadi, who knew his true identity, told him to get a grip and make a move.

"She can only say no," Skadi's airy statement, no help whatsoever.

"Try me." Xavier held his breath, willing Anna to follow her heart, even knowing she had yet to acknowledge the latent sentiment lurking there.

Anna looked at him, dubiously. About to dismiss his request and make a joke, something in his eyes... his fathomless, midnight-blue eyes... froze the words before they tumbled over her lips.

With a resigned shrug, she sighed, "My life is a mess."

"Because?"

Anna glanced around the diner. The pictures adorning the walls spoke of an eccentric mind.

Should I risk the truth, or am I opening myself up to ridicule?

Her heart assumed control and she burst out, "I am the most powerful being in the universe. I dispatched Odin the Asgardian when I was nine, then the cretin was revived by a misguided valkyrie and I had to fight him again.

"My parents are gods, I shared my soul with another deity, my adopted aunt used to rule Fólkvangr, and her husband may or may not be a Crow medicine man.

"As if that isn't enough, despite my best efforts be interested, anthropology is the most boring subject known to man, unless you are actually in the field, which means I wasted half this semester and will probably have to change majors. I don't know what I'm going to do."

Anna rattled this off too quickly for comprehension, but her listener was well-versed in incoherence; at this time of night, most of his customers were far from sober.

She saw his lips twitch.

You take the mick or ask whether I'm drunk, and I'm outta here.

Her brows knitted and, mentally, she palmed her forehead.

Couldn't just say school sucks, could you? Noooooo, you had to spout all that nonsense. Way to ruin a friendship.

"Our friendship is not ruined," Xavier interrupted Anna's self-recrimination.

Startled, her head shot up, and her gaze collided with his.

"Did I say that out loud?"

"You did not."

"So..."

"I already know everything about you. I was starting to think you would never tell me."

Anna narrowed her eyes. "You know everything about me? Hang on, is this some kind of set up? Skadi?" she hollered, glaring around the restaurant, which, bizarrely... given the time of night... was still empty.

Xavier chuckled. "Skadi is not here, it is just you and me. Perhaps I ought to introduce myself. The name is Baldr."

Speechless, Anna tried to decide whether this was some monumental, and not very funny, joke.

Xavier was not laughing, and his expression told her he was serious.

Anna's jaw dropped. The silence stretched out and she just stared at him, a reply refusing to form.

Then...

"B-Baldr? As in Freya's son, Baldr?" Her voice shot up an octave. "Wait... oh, my god, is my mother behind this? Have you been spying on me?"

Stunned, Anna gesticulated wildly, almost smacking Xavier in the face.

He seized her hands and dragged her close. "No one is spying on you," his voice dropped to a growl. "I confess, this was just a job when I started here, but then we met and now all I can think of is doing this..."

He kissed her.

Anna felt she ought to slap him into next week...

Talk about taking liberties.

...except *the* most exquisite sensation started. An intoxicating glissade from the top of her spine to the tip of her toes, coiling out along her veins.

When, finally, Xavier... Baldr... lifted his head, she was glassy eyed and gasping.

"Okay, we definitely need to talk about this, but first..." she pinned him with her shrewd gaze.

"First?" He quirked a brow.

"Do that again.

He did!

EPILOGUE

Five years later

H ands on hips, Anna Helsdatter surveyed her surroundings. She was standing in front of Old Main, the oldest building on campus and the first building, in what was then Dakota territory, specifically constructed as an institution for higher education.

Its beauty never failed to take her breath away and she would miss seeing it every day... although...

Her thoughts winged to Baldr.

Following that sublime kiss, she had punched him in the gut and demanded full disclosure.

His explanation, which irked her initially, tempting her to drive through the night to the ranch, to deliver an earbashing to her family, made sense... albeit convoluted.

"Mother only proposed the notion because your parents were so concerned. She thought it was better for me to keep an eye on you than have them drop in every time you blew your nose."

Baldr's knowing grin, tugged a responding one from Anna.

She *did* discuss this unexpected development with Skadi, mindful the goddess once held a candle for Baldr.

Even thinking about dating someone for whom your best friend, not to mention erstwhile soul-sister, once, and maybe still, bore a profound affection, broke a hard and fast, if unwritten, rule.

As she had when the subject of Anna dating Xavier was first broached, Skadi dispelled her concerns.

"Hon, that was millennia ago. I told you dark brooding types don't float my boat. Now, if you were interested in that hunk of muscle on the Nordic combined team, we might have an issue..." Skadi had grinned wickedly.

Her family did not get off scot-free but, by the time she went home, Anna's pique had dwindled.

Being courted — because that's exactly what Baldr was doing... his old-fashioned manners, far more seductive than the *wham bam thank you ma'am* her peers seemed to get a buzz out of — left no room for indignation, however righteous.

Not only that, and umbrage aside, her lecture faltered at the first hurdle when, as she crossed the threshold into the ranch, her father waved a glass of mead under her nose and her mother placed a bowl of Irish strew in front of her.

With a wry smile and warm hugs, Anna gave up — the ticking off could wait... was it really that important? — and allowed herself to be cosseted, acknowledging her parents had only ever wanted her safe and happy.

She blew a sigh and turned, walking smack bang into something solid.

"Murph..." she muttered against a broad chest.

"Hello to you too," an amused voice spoke above her, and a kiss was brushed to the top of her head.

Anna looked up into Baldr's beautiful eyes.

She didn't care that referring to any part of the male anatomy as beautiful was deemed politically incorrect, in her opinion, his eyes were quite breathtakingly beautiful. They twinkled whenever he looked at her and seemed to hold the universe in their depths.

Anna, *the* authority on all things Norse, knew the sagas word for word, and the attributes ascribed to Baldr — light, wisdom, and courage — sat well with her.

These same sagas cited the goddess, Nanna, as his wife and, while Baldr and she were not yet wed, or even close to being betrothed, Anna took impish delight in the knowledge that, sometimes, ancient scribes got their spelling wrong. A mistake, she had no intention of correcting.

"You ready?" Baldr asked, entwining their fingers. "We have work to do."

"As I'll ever be." Anna smiled, the familiar thrill trickling through her. A thrill which had intensified the longer they were together.

There was no doubt in her mind that they were destined to meet, that everything in her life, which had spanned more than the last twenty four years, had led to their first encounter.

As the most powerful being in the Nine Realms and beyond, Anna had responsibilities she could not avoid but, she was extremely good at delegating.

A somewhat riotous conference with the surviving pantheon had resulted in a number of changes.

The main one being that Valhalla, believed doomed after Odin's treachery, was resurrected, under the proviso it was run by a committee instead of one god.

So far, following a smooth transition, the arrangement had proven to be a success.

Other than paying an occasional call, Anna left it to the new management, and concentrated on being a student.

Skadi had one semester left, and Sela had implied they would keep the apartment as an investment property, should the girls no longer require it.

Now all her hard work was over and she wondered what the next chapter of her life would bring. She hoped it featured the tall, dark, and ruggedly handsome deity holding her hand but she wasn't game to assume... despite what it said in the sagas.

They strolled towards Bug, chatting about nothing of any great importance.

Anna's newly minted double masters opened the doors to numerous careers, but she had a yearning to take some time off to — what was it people said? — sit back and smell the roses.

The last four years had been challenging, draining, exhausting, fulfilling, and exciting... and that was just the course. Throw in several shocking revelations about your ancestry, four murders... although three of the bodies had never been found... and a deadly battle with a crazed god — surely no one begrudged her an extended holiday.

They drove to the diner in comfortable silence. Another facet of Baldr's character which endeared Anna to him was, unless circumstance dictated, he was a man of few words, and never felt the need to shatter a quiet moment with unnecessary conversation.

Baldr unlocked the door, but instead of opening it, turned to Anna, as ever struck by her astonishing beauty. She quite took his breath away, totally unaware this was the exact same reaction Loki had every time he looked at Anna's mother.

One of which, his soon to be father-in-law, had anyone predicted the next few moments, would approve.

"So, Ms. Helsdatter, what are your plans?"

Anna shrugged, "Right at this moment, blueberry pancakes and iced coffee."

"And after that?"

"Hibernation." She winked.

"I have a proposal."

Anna waited.

The balmy air of the June afternoon seemed to sizzle in anticipation.

"You have a masters and are probably raring to change the world. I have a diner with plenty of loyal customers, and have grown rather fond of both.

"We are blessed, or cursed, with being deities, although currently only working at that part time, granting us ridiculous amounts of power, which we, of course, never ever abuse.

"How about, I keep the home fires burning or, and more pertinently, the griddles hot, while you save the planet, or one of the other Realms. I love you more than life itself, but the last thing I want to do is clip your wings."

"What if I have lost the desire to fly?" Anna sounded uncharacteristically shy.

Relieved his intuition could be trusted, Baldr slid a gentle finger under Anna's chin and tilted her face until their eyes locked.

"Then, perhaps you might consider signing up as a casual waitress? I know a wonderful guy who could use your expertise."

"Hmmm, your... *the guy's,* terms?" Enjoying the game, Anna's lips started to curve.

"It is a lifetime commitment, involving a ring, fiery

passion, lazy mornings in bed, late nights under the stars and maybe one or two kids," Baldr replied nonchalantly.

Anna tapped her chin, thoughtfully. "I am sorely tempted. Do you, by any chance, have an example of these terms?"

"This ought to persuade you."

Baldr whisked her into his arms.

His kiss went on and on and on, promising a lifetime... an eternity... of love and laughter, of spirited debate and peaceful interludes, of joys and sorrows, and of coming home to each other.

Valhalla's Doom had become Anna's liberation, and she was not about to waste a single moment.

She grinned, and it lit her face.

"When do I start?"

About the Author

RORI BLEU

With a smattering of riverboat pirates and royalty in her heritage, Rori Bleu's childhood reflected her past.
An interest in fairy tales, myth and legend were as important as spirited discussions around politics and current affairs — although some might argue they are one and the same!

A fascination, sparked by listening to Grimm's Fairy Tales at her grandmother's knee, not only encouraged Rori's passion for reading, but also steered her into the world of RPG's.
What began as a fun pastime, soon evolved into the creation of fantastical worlds, but Rori never lost her love of politics going on to specialise in Governmental History and Historical Research.

Naturally this means her stories are steeped in historical accuracy and real-life intrigue. While Rori's love of a happily ever after means her preferred genre is romance, don't be surprised if you discover an occasional detour into historical fiction, thrillers, horror and fantasy.

To find more of Rori's books... click the link
https://linktr.ee/roribleu

f

About the Author
ROSIE CHAPEL

Rosie Chapel lives in Perth, Australia with her hubby and two furkids. When not writing, she loves catching up with friends, burying herself in a book (or three), discovering the wonders of Western Australia, or — and the best — a quiet evening at home with her husband, enjoying a glass of wine and a movie.

Website: www.rosiechapel.com

Also by Rori Bleu

Pineapple Meringue

Imprisoned Hearts

Port of London

Dani's Masquerade

Black Tulips

Ajei's Destiny

Porta Aeternum

The Queen's Heart

Syn *with Matthew Forester*

With Rosie Chapel

Echoes and Illusions

Evie's War

Vindicta

Corrupt Covenant

Lesser of Two Evils

The Sela Helsdatter Saga - with Rosie Chapel

A Flip of The Coin - Book One

Conceived Chaos - Book Two

Odin's Bane - Book Three

Valhalla's Doom - Book Four

Arcane Alchemy: Freya's Fate - *A Helsdatter Saga Novella*

Also by Rosie Chapel

<u>Historical Fiction</u>

The Hannah's Heirloom Sequence

The Pomegranate Tree - Book One

Echoes of Stone and Fire - Book Two

Embers of Destiny - Book Three

Etched in Starlight - Prequel

Hannah's Heirloom Trilogy - Compilation — e-book only

Prelude to Fate

Legacy of Flame and Ash

The Nettleby Trilogy (WW1 Novellas)

A Guardian Unexpected - Book One

Under the Clock - Book Two

Evie's War *with Rori Bleu*

Vindicta *with Rori Bleu*

Corrupt Covenant - *with Rori Bleu*

Lesser of Two Evils - *with Rori Bleu*

The Sela Helsdatter Saga with Rori Bleu

A Flip of The Coin - Book One

Conceived Chaos - Book Two

Odin's Bane - Book Three

Valhalla's Doom - Book Four

Arcane Alchemy: Freya's Fate - *A Helsdatter Saga Novella*

Regency Romances

The Linen and Lace Series

Once Upon An Earl - Book One

To Unlock Her Heart - Book Two

Love on a Winter's Tide - Book Three

A Love Unquenchable - Book Four

A Hidden Rose — Book Five

An Unexpected Romance

Elusive Hearts - Book One

Shrouded Hearts - Book Two

The Daffodil Garden

The Unconventional Duchess

Rescuing Her Knight - *the de Wiltons:* Book One

His Fiery Hoyden

A Regency Duet

A Regency Christmas Double

Fate is Curious

A Christmas Prayer *with Ashlee Shades*

The Lady's Wager

Winning Emma

A Love Impossible

Unravelling Roana

Love Kindled

Moonbeams and Mistletoe

Fairy Tale Romance

Chasing Bluebells

Contemporary Romances

Of Ruins and Romance

All At Once It's You

Cobweb Dreams

Just One Step

His Heart's Second Sigh

Dystopian Romance

Echoes & Illusions *with Rori Bleu*

9 781763 540705